DATE DUE

JAN 5 2009		

D0098910

WITHDRAWN

Property of:
Hall Middle School Library
200 Doherty Drive
Larkspur, CA 94939

Louisiana's Song

KERRY MADDEN

VIKING

VIKING
Published by Penguin Group
Penguin Young Readers Group, 345 Hudson Street, New York, New York 10014, U.S.A.
Penguin Group (Canada), 90 Eglinton Avenue East, Suite 700, Toronto, Ontario,
Canada M4P 2Y3 (a division of Pearson Penguin Canada Inc.)
Penguin Books Ltd, 80 Strand, London WC2R 0RL, England
Penguin Ireland, 25 St Stephen's Green, Dublin 2, Ireland (a division of Penguin Books Ltd)
Penguin Group (Australia), 250 Camberwell Road, Camberwell, Victoria 3124, Australia
(a division of Pearson Australia Group Pty Ltd)
Penguin Books India Pvt Ltd, 11 Community Centre, Panchsheel Park, New Delhi – 110 017, India
Penguin Group (NZ), 67 Apollo Drive, Mairangi Bay, Auckland 1311, New Zealand
(a division of Pearson New Zealand Ltd)
Penguin Books (South Africa) (Pty) Ltd, 24 Sturdee Avenue, Rosebank, Johannesburg 2196,
South Africa

Penguin Books Ltd, Registered Offices: 80 Strand, London WC2R 0RL, England

First published in 2007 by Viking, a division of Penguin Young Readers Group

10 9 8 7 6 5 4 3 2 1

Copyright © Kerry Madden, 2007
All rights reserved

LIBRARY OF CONGRESS CATALOGING-IN-PUBLICATION DATA IS AVAILABLE
ISBN: 978-0-670-06153-2

Printed in the U.S.A.
Set in Granjon

For Ernestine E. Upchurch,
who bloomed where she was planted in Maggie Valley.

For Caroline Burnette,
a born storyteller if there ever was one!

And always for Kiffen,
and
for Flannery, Lucy, and Norah . . .

And in memory of
Iris Elizabeth Teague Lunsford,
a mountain woman of grace, kindness, and laughter

"In a dark time,
the eye begins to see."

—Theodore Roethke

~ Contents ~

CHAPTER ONE

Shades of Blue

Ghost Town in the Sky
May 1, 1963

Dear Livy Two,
Here is ten dollars. It's all I got this week. Uncle Buddy
"borrowed" the rest of my paycheck to pay his poker debts
but aims to pay me back. WARNING: DO NOT blab
to Mama or Grandma Horace about poker. Guess what?
We saw this Al Hitchcock movie called The Birds *over in*
Asheville with a bunch of Ghost Town folks, but it scared
Uncle Buddy so bad he had to step outside to smoke a
cigarette in the middle. Now he watches the sky for killer
birds.
Daddy back home yet?
Love, your brother, Emmett
P.S. I expect to be permoted from merry-go-round man

to bona fide gunslinger any day now, and then I'll look like a true outlaw from the Wild West, scaring the living tar out of all those South Carolina terists, making jail breaks, jumping from the roof of the bank. And P.S. again, send up some more Adventure Comics *from the bookmobile. I need to read up on Saturn Girl, Lightning Lad, and Chameleon Boy.*

Emmett sure sounds happier these days than he did living at home with us. Does he miss us at all? Not a minute, probably.

"You done in the smokehouse yet, Louise?" I hang by my legs up in the red maple tree. World looks funny upside down, with all the blood in my body rushing straight to my head. "Please, Louise? I'll let you read Emmett's letter!" No answer. "Louisiana Weems! Answer me! You been in there *forever*!" My eleven-year-old sister hates to be called "Louisiana," which is only her real name.

"Livy Two! Livy Two!" The twins, Caroline and Cyrus, age four, and Gentle, three, prowl the back holler hunting me, but I stay hidden in the spring leaves. Gentle and Caroline wear fairy wings, but Cyrus is dressed up like King Tut. He's as wild for mummies as Caroline and Gentle are for fairies. They want me to play with them, but I want to be alone a little longer before I got to start watching kids again. Gentle listens hard and knows every inch of the holler and don't let being blind stop her at nothing. Emmett whittled her a little cane too, and she uses it all the time except when she's climbing trees, and I taught her to climb trees good as the twins now. But since her hearing is razor sharp, I know soon enough she'll direct the twins to my hiding spot. Our sausage-shaped dog, Uncle Hazard, races after them all howling, *Barrooo! Barrooo!*

Gentle yells, "Livy Two! Livy Two!"

Caroline calls, "When are we going up to Waterrock Knob? The fairy place?"

Cyrus shouts, "Yeah, you promised! Where are you anyhow?"

I play possum. Waterrock Knob sits at the top of the Plott Balsams, over six thousand feet high, and I do aim to take the little ones up there real soon. Folks say you can see Georgia, South Carolina, and some of East Tennessee from the top. If the truth be told, I'm so dadgummed sick of babysitting I could scream. I'm itching to get out and see the world more than ever, but I can't say that to Mama or Grandma Horace, what with Daddy coming home today for the first time in eight months since the car wreck last August. I look again for a hint of movement from the smokehouse. "Louise! Time's up! No fooling! Can't hide in there forever! Time to show us your masterpiece, girl."

Nothing.

The landlady's skinny cow, Bony Birdy Sweetpea, drowses by the fence behind the smokehouse, swishing at flies with her tail. The little ones named her 'cause the only name she ever had before was "Cow" and 'cause of her spare frame. Mama buys Bony Birdy Sweetpea salt bricks and cow feed from the general store down the road called the "Maggie Store," but nothing seems to fatten her up. Me and Louise take turns milking her, but Becksie and Jitters won't touch milking a cow—not for all the tea in China—and Grandma Horace says she don't blame them. I chop the wood, too, and catch fish now that Emmett lives up at Ghost Town in the Sky. Shoot, I'd rather chop wood and fish than sweep a floor any day.

I try to read an E. E. Cummings poem upside down called "Buffalo Bill's" about a "watersmooth-silver stallion" and a "blue-eyed boy," but I can't concentrate a lick. Sometimes, it makes me dizzy reading and hanging upside down. Still, I can do it for longer than anybody in all of Haywood County and probably Buncombe County too. I flip back upright and stick the book inside the wooden crate that I've hammered to the tree where I keep all my song notebooks. I got a piece of tin over it, so it won't get wet, case it rains.

I study the May sky, which is pure cobalt—the kind

of blue you can get lost in if you stare hard enough. As the painter in the family, Louise aims to teach us the best ways to describe certain colors.

"Hey, Louise," I yell down to her, "what are all those shades of blue again?"

She hollers out the window, "How many times I got to tell you? Azure, sapphire, indigo, cerulean, turquoise, midnight, navy, robin's egg, ocean—and that's just to start!"

"Well, that's enough! Come on, one peek?"

"No, now quit!"

Inside the house, Becksie and Jitters watch Appelonia and baby Tom-Bill, our new baby brother, born almost a month ago. This is Mama's first day away from him. I wonder if Daddy will even recognize Appelonia, who calls to mind a spider monkey like they have in the Yucatan the way she grabs at everything. She can't walk yet but scoots everywhere on her bottom, collecting acorns and whatnot in her cotton diaper. Becksie and Jitters's idea of babysitting is pounding on the old piano that Grandma Horace saved from the Methodists. To entertain (or torture) the babies, they slam out hymns like "Will the Circle Be Unbroken" and "Uncloudy Day." Uncle Hazard stops running to stand outside the window and howl *Barrooo! Barrooo!* accompanying the piano playing, on tune too.

We got the piano because the Methodist church down in Enka-Stinka was fixing to throw it out, but since Grandma Horace had donated it to them years ago, she made them haul it up here to Maggie Valley. She did it for Gentle, who likes to sing and find her own songs on the keys like she's trying to uncover secrets. Gentle's voice makes folks stop whatever they're doing just to listen. Me, I got a down-home singing voice that I know folks like, but Mama says Gentle's voice comes from a holy place.

I wish Daddy'd get here already. At the crack of dawn, Mathew the Mennonite picked up Mama and Grandma Horace in his black truck and drove them to Asheville to collect him from the Rip Van Winkle rest home. My heart is like to bust with this magic day of Daddy on his way home. It means life will finally get back to normal around here. I creep up higher to another branch until I'm part of the wind blowing in the eagle's nest of the tree, but I'm warm in one of Mama's sweaters she knitted me. I get a view of the spring-green mountains showered with snowy azalea blossoms, lavender forget-me-nots, bloodroot, mayapples, chickweed, and dogwoods. The kudzu vines loop and curl around the trees to make giant shapes that resemble drowsing dinosaurs.

"Livy Two, Livy Two!" Cyrus and Caroline and Gentle are back again calling and calling—just a few more minutes and then I swear I'll play with them. I inch out farther on the branch to spy on Louise. When the little ones scramble into the house to look for me, I call to Louise again in a more urgent whisper. "Louisiana Margaret Pansy Jeanne Marie Weems! You can't hide in there forever. One peek!"

"Hold your horses, Livy Two!" My sister can paint for hours on end without a break, and no itchy distractions from the real world can drag her back for love or money. Daddy and Mama gave her the name of a state and a slew of middle names, because they liked how it all sounded together. Louise swears she's going to the Haywood County judge over at the courthouse in Waynesville when she's old enough to get rid of a few. I know she'd also like to ask him if he could make her shorter, too, since she's grown so dang tall this year. I think she is lucky to be tall, but she tells me I have no idea what it feels like to be a giraffe girl in a crowd of Lilliputians. Her being so tall is what has made her so shy of strangers, mainly because folks always feel the need to comment on her height. *"Aren't you a nice tall girl?"* or *"Got enough oxygen up there?"*

I see her hand polishing the windows of Daddy's new home. Mathew the Mennonite cut out a picture window in the smokehouse, so Daddy will have plenty of light. The window is level, but since the smokehouse has settled over the years, it looks si-goggling with the tin roof slanted off at an angle, resembling a lean-to log house.

Daddy woke up more than a month ago. Finally! They had to do a lot of memory games and exercises with him, but now he is truly awake, and the doctor said it was all right for him to come home. The beginning of a song weaves its way into my brain—I've been writing down all my songs and intend to send them to the music men in Nashville, so I can make some money to help the family. I also listen to Patsy Cline's songs whenever I can find them on the radio. She's barely been dead two months, and I still can't believe it. I miss her like she was my own blood. She fought to get into Music City USA herself, just like I aim to do, because I want to be a singer too.

But first we need money real bad. Grandma Horace calls us a bunch of squander-birds without two nickels to rub together and likes to say, "I know we've experienced some tragedies as of late, but I wish my mountain grandchildren would understand that I am not an open pocketbook full of greenback dollars."

It's terrible to always be thinking of making ends meet, but I can't help it. I don't want to go to the poorhouse. I play the notes to a new song on my guitar. The feel of the strings and wood beneath my fingers makes it all okay even when it's not.

Shades of Blue

We'll be blue if you send us to the poorhouse,
Azure, sapphire, and aquamarine.
I know we'll be blue in the poorhouse,
Midnight, turquoise, and cerulean.
If you don't take us to the poorhouse,
Navy, robin's egg, and ocean,
We'll never be blue again.

"That is one plain awful song." Becksie stands under the tree peering up at me, with Gentle, who has discovered me just like I knew she would. Jitters, Appelonia, and Tom-Bill are there too.

"Yep, your worst one yet!" says Jitters, the mountain echo.

"You two priss-pots think of a better one!" I snap at the dirty spies.

Becksie wags a finger, saying, "Songwriting doesn't put food on the table! It's high time you came down and helped us with these kids! We got chores to do! And I got to work on my poster and speech for my Maggie Queen competition."

"Yeah!" Jitters says. "And I'm her royal helper."

"Royal slave is more like. And do y'all think the queen competition puts food on the table? You think Harriet

Tubman ran for school queen? Or Eleanor Roosevelt?"

"Too bad for them!" Becksie snaps. "I am running, and I aim to win too!"

The smokehouse door bangs open and Louise says, "Y'all quit. Don't fight on Daddy's homecoming day. Come on in and have a look." Louise wipes at a smear of homemade purple paint on her face, mixed from gypsum clay and blackberries. Her thick mane of strawberry-blonde hair twists into a long ponytail down her back.

The twins and Gentle are already at the smokehouse door with Uncle Hazard, and I scale down the tree to join them. Bony Birdy Sweetpea moans a low moo like she'd like to come along too, but then I realize it's because a rumbling engine has caught her ear. Mathew the Mennonite's truck grinds up into the holler with Daddy riding in a wheelchair strapped in the flatbed, Mama right next to him. The little ones look toward the truck waving and calling, "Daddy! Hey, Daddy! Over here!"

A thrill of joy sparks through me, but when I look closer, I get a lump in my throat. The daddy in the flat-bed wears pajamas and a brown bathrobe and sits real still—not waving or looking at us the way he used to when he'd come into the holler. What's the matter with him? He's supposed to be fine now. The daddy in my head doesn't match the one in front of me.

CHAPTER TWO

Invisible Kid

ME AND LOUISE find ourselves holding hands—tight, sweaty fingers curled around each other while we wait for Daddy to sit up straight and snap out of it. I whisper, "We ain't seen what you painted yet," and she says, "Never mind about it. It's all right."

I look toward the smokehouse, and from the open doorway, a glow of color fills the air with ghostly hues of sapphire and yellow-gold. What will Daddy think when he looks up and sees his new home? But he doesn't move from the wheelchair. He is hunched forward in his bathrobe, and his shoulder blades stick out like broke bird wings. Mama climbs down to hug the little ones, but also to shoo them off from swarming up on him too fast. Grandma Horace sits up front with Mathew the Mennonite. Daddy don't notice the banner that hangs from the front porch that says, WELCOME

HOME, DADDY! He doesn't seem even the least little bit excited, but maybe he's just tired out. Uncle Hazard growls and barks at him like he's some outlander.

"Why is Daddy back there in the flatbed?" Worry-wart Jitters skitters around the truck in her pin curlers. "And not in the cab? He could have fallen out and bounced down the road!"

"Your daddy's been inside for so long he wanted some fresh air," Mama explains. "Isn't that right, Tom?"

"Well, my back hurts." Grandma Horace hoists herself out of the cab. "What I have endured for this family, what I have endured . . . I hope someone has taken note."

"Daddy, you're home!" Becksie shifts Appelonia on her hip, attempting to pull out her pin curlers. "But we're not ready. Me and Jitters tried to curl our hair up pretty for you." Appelonia grabs fistfuls of Becksie's hair, which sends Becksie further into orbit. "Appelonia! You're messing it up with your sticky baby hands!"

Daddy watches us with mild interest like we might be some stranger family he's not come across before. Then he looks around him and asks, "What is this place?"

My stomach gets cold at that question. Cyrus and Gentle yell, "Home! Home! Howdy, Daddy!" their little voices quick with joy. A glint of fear crosses Caroline's face, and she cries, "That man is scary." Grandma

Horace hushes her up, but Caroline is right. Daddy is scary. His skin looks pale, like he's been indoors for too long. I stay away from the fuss around Mathew the Mennonite's truck. Baby Tom-Bill wails, and Louise picks him up from his basket and cuddles him close, so he quits his fussing. She walks the baby over to the truck and says, "Meet baby Tom-Bill, Daddy."

I steal up behind her. "We think he looks like a cross between Emmett and Grandma Horace. What do you think, Daddy?" He doesn't hear me, so I inch a little closer to see what he'll think of the new baby. Louise sets the baby on Daddy's lap in the wheelchair. Daddy pats him, and Tom-Bill grabs Daddy's finger. Then Mama reaches for Tom-Bill, and our baby clings to her. He and Daddy share near the same expressions on their faces—pure worry.

"I'm dressed like a mummy, Daddy!" Cyrus shows Daddy his arms draped in strips of cloth. "I don't think you're scary, Daddy. Are you?"

When he doesn't answer Cyrus, Caroline hangs back like she's afraid to get too close. Gentle feels her way along the truck and climbs toward Daddy's lap, but he doesn't look at her. She finds his lap and plays with his hair with her fingers. "Daddy got a haircut. It's short."

"It's a flattop," Mama says to nobody. "It's the style,

according to the barber at the home. He gets the patients spruced up before they turn them loose."

"Get down, Gentle!" Becksie helps her down off the truck. "I swear these children don't know how to behave, do they?" Her voice sounds forced.

Grandma Horace speaks in her matter-of-fact way, "Now I want you children to stand back and give the man some breathing room. We got us a long row to hoe."

Mama says, "Tom, look here at everybody. They're all here except for Emmett, who's still got that job at Ghost Town."

"Emmett sent ten dollars," I blurt out. "In a letter. Today. I got it."

Daddy says suddenly, "Emmett's here? Where?"

"No, no . . . he's up at Ghost Town in the Sky," Becksie tells him.

"Ten dollars? Is that all? Lord, Lord." Grandma Horace blows her nose and sees us staring hard at Daddy. "Now, children, you're not to be afraid. Your daddy got a good knock in the head last year, but he'll come back around by and by."

I try to swallow the hard knot in my throat.

Gentle says, "Is Daddy gonna stay home forever and ever now?" But then Daddy starts crying, shucking sobs like he can't catch his breath, and nobody knows what to do.

"It ain't what I thought. It ain't what I thought." He swipes at the tears on his face.

Me either, is what I think but don't say.

Cyrus says, "Whatcha crying for, Daddy?"

Caroline yanks her sweater up over her head so she won't have to look at him. Instead of this being the miracle day of Daddy home, it's something else that makes me want to hide or at least turn back time.

Grandma Horace says, "Good Lord, Tom, behave yourself! You're home in Maggie Valley and these are your children." She turns back to us. "The doctor says we need to explain things to your daddy, even what might seem plain as day to most folk, because his memory is pure befuddlement." She rubs her hands like she's scrubbing them with invisible soap. "Pure befuddlement."

Finally, Mama says, "Tom, I think you need a good nap. It was a long trip. Do you want to have Mr. Mathew wheel you over to the smokehouse?"

"What for? My head hurts. I got a headache."

"I'll get you some aspirin. The smokehouse is all fixed up for you."

"What for?"

Grandma Horace gets fed up quick with this line of questioning and says, "Tom Weems, do you want to recover what's left of your battered wits in a house of nine children, ten if you count when Emmett visits? I am losing mine by the minute with so many underfoot, but I shall not dwell. Children, we need to all pitch in and get your daddy's memory up to snuff again."

Becksie dives right in with, "I'll help! Daddy, who is the president?"

Daddy studies Becksie before he says, "FDR."

"No, Daddy! Wrong!" my big sister trumpets like a no-nonsense school marm. "It's John F. Kennedy, and his wife is Jackie Kennedy. Their kids are Caroline and John-John. You brought us home that *LIFE* magazine of their pictures that one time? Remember, Daddy?"

"Remember, Daddy?" Jitters tugs on his sleeve. "What year is it? Remember?"

"Remember, remember!" I snap at them. "Would y'all quit and let him catch his breath without giving him a current-events lesson before he's got out of the truck?"

Mathew the Mennonite slides two boards out of the back for the wheelchair and helps wheel Daddy off the flatbed and onto the ground.

"Are you all better now, Daddy?" Cyrus hangs on the back of the wheelchair.

From under her sweater, Caroline repeats, "That man with the headache is scary."

Becksie pulls Caroline's sweater back down and warns, "Caroline Weems, you quit saying that now or I'll scare you myself." Naturally this makes Caroline hiccup into tears, but she swallows them and balls her hands into tight fists at her sides. I wish I could call upon the mountain fairies to turn back time.

Mathew the Mennonite says, "Mr. Weems? May I push your chair for you?"

Grandma Horace says, "There's no need to be asking his permission." Her voice is bossy, but her glass eye, the color of chestnut today, seems to behold our sadness. Grandma Horace's different colored glass eyes always seem to catch our moods or hers.

Daddy speaks up in a low, scratchy voice, "I want to walk, I want to walk!"

"That's fine, Tom." Mama squeezes his hand, but he doesn't look at her.

"And somebody turn off that radio." He glances around him.

"What radio?" Gentle wants to know. "The radio's not playing, Daddy."

"Most certainly is. Got a Carter Family tune busting in my ears." Daddy shakes his head like he's trying to shake out the sound.

Mama says, "I'll turn it down, Tom. Children, sometimes your daddy hears music that we can't hear. The doctors call it 'auditory hallucinations.'"

Cyrus yells, "Hey, I want to have auditorium hallucinates too!"

"Auditory hallucinations! Doctor says it's like he's got

a radio in his head." Grandma Horace adds, "If you ever heard of such a foolish notion, which I have not!"

A radio in his head? I wonder what other songs he hears playing. We all hold our breath as Daddy puts his legs on the ground. He looks around at all our faces for a split second and seems about to say something but changes his mind. I try not to cry when he looks right through me like I might be Invisible Kid from one of Emmett's comics. Mama nods to Mathew the Mennonite, and carefully, he helps Daddy walk up the steep path toward the smokehouse. We follow along behind him. But halfway there, Daddy shakes off all help. "Thank you very much, I can do it! Is it this way?" He drips beads of sweat as he lurches toward the smokehouse.

When he arrives at the steps to the smokehouse after an eternity, Mama says to us kids, "That's far enough. Your daddy needs to rest. You'll have plenty of time to visit with him later."

But we don't want to wait until later. We been waiting long enough.

CHAPTER THREE

Buttermilk Moon

AS WE KEEP walking toward the smokehouse, ignoring Mama, Becksie smiles like she's the world's fairy godmother and announces, "Me and Jitters made a stack cake—eight layers, with lots of mashed dried apples between each layer."

"Yep, one of his favorites!" Jitters nods. "It used to be anyway. Is it still one of your favorites, Daddy? 'Cause we can make another kind if you want."

Grandma Horace pats Jitters, ordering, "Hush, Myrtle Anne." She turns to Mama and says, "Jessie, I'll take the baby to the house." Grandma Horace scoops up baby Tom-Bill from Mama and heads across the yard.

As Mama pushes open the door to the smokehouse, Daddy steps inside, and we crowd around the doorway without crossing the threshold. It smells of fresh paint. The meat hooks still hang from the ceiling, but from the hooks hang branches of pine and cedar and bunches of dog hobble to combat the new-paint smell. It's truly like a whole other world now because of Louise's paint-brush.

Gentle, who sniffs the air, says, "What did Louise paint? Tell me the pictures."

I try to take it in with my eyes, but it's hard to breathe in all at once, so I tell her, "It's all of us, Gentle. Over on this wall is a big painting—of fairies in all their fairy houses at the top of Waterrock Knob. That's Caroline's part. Right, Louise?"

Louise nods, but then Mama says, "Look, Tom, there's Emmett's wall with a harmonica and a whittling knife. And here is a chairlift that disappears into the clouds above the mountains. There he is being a gun-slinger at Ghost Town."

Becksie cries, "It's me and Jitters square-dancing for the Queen of England like the Soco Dance Team of Maggie did when Mrs. Eleanor Roosevelt invited them!"

"I look so beautiful!" Jitters two-steps in the smoke-house and crashes into the desk, knocking over a bowl of apples for Daddy. "Sorry! Sorry! Don't be mad!" She scrambles around on the floor picking up apples. Cyrus leaps up and down, shouting, "Hey, I found me. Me and Gentle and Caroline are collecting bugs by Jonathan Creek. And look there—King Tut in his sarcophagus! Boy-howdy! See, Daddy, see me!"

Caroline cries, "And Uncle Hazard's chasing butter-flies by his pinecone palace."

Daddy's eyes seem to drink up everything, but his face is impossible to read. The old Daddy would have talked a blue streak about his brilliant artist daughter. "What is this place?" he wants to know.

"Your home, Tom," Mama tells him. "You live here."

"Not me!"

Nobody contradicts him, but he is so home! Where else would he be? How are we supposed to get used to this new Daddy? I look at a painting of me feed-ing Uncle Hazard apples, his favorite treat—a funny treat for a dog, but that's Uncle Hazard. In the paint-ing, we're sitting smack next to a rainbow that arcs way up over Setzer Mountain and disappears. I study the smokehouse walls some more, because something bugs me about the mural, and then I see what I don't see. I turn to Louise and ask, "Why aren't you in the paint-ings?"

Louise shrugs. "I don't know. Can't paint myself, I reckon."

"But you ought to put yourself in with all of us. You could be in a corner wearing watermelon shoes or painting your peahens on a wheelbarrow or whistling one of your famous, ear-piercing whistles. Something like that?"

Louise gets quiet, and her face turns the color of her reddish hair. It's clear that she don't want any opinions about her smokehouse art.

"Louise?"

"You sing your songs the way you want, and I don't say a thing. So just leave me be to paint my pictures the way I see them." Louise's voice trembles. "Good gosh, everybody always has an opinion in this family."

"Well, sorry!" My sensitive sister is like to bust out crying all over the place.

Mama steps between us, putting her arms around Louise. "You've done some miracles in this place. These pictures are going to be a comfort to Daddy. They already are to me." She admires a sunrise over Uncle Hazard's pinecone palace. "And look, there is Emmett's rock collection from when he was a boy. You didn't forget a thing."

On the window ledge sits a string of Emmett's rocks all lined up in a neat, polished row. Once, a long time ago, Daddy took us to the Nantahala River Gem Mine over in Bryson City, and we dug for hours in the dirt to find stones with shovels and buckets. And Emmett collected all kinds of stones as a kid: moonstones, quartz, tiger's-eye, jade, amethyst, garnet, topaz . . . He taught me the names, but I guess he forgot about the stones. Daddy's banjo leans against the wall, and I sure hope he feels like picking on it later.

"Where'd you find Emmett's rocks?" Cyrus examines each one after another.

"In a shoe box in the barn."

Caroline points. "Look, Gentle's picking flowers with fairies swirling around her head too. And look, there's a dolphin swimming in the creek 'cause Louise loves dolphins. But there's no dolphins in these mountains. It's just in Louise's head."

Gentle says, "I feel fairy wings on my face every single day!" Then she hums "Wildwood Flower," and her voice is so pretty.

But as Mama helps Daddy to bed, he shouts, "The radio's giving me a headache. Holy Moses. Turn it down! There's a crowd."

Mama's hands are shaking, so Mathew the Mennonite motions for us to follow him out the door. We leave, but then sneak around to the side window.

Inside the smokehouse, Mama says, "I expect you're tired now, aren't you? Now I want you to sleep, Tom. Clean sheets all ready for you. It took near forever, but I saved up three books of green stamps and bought new sheets from the redemption store." Mama loves her S & H green stamps and carefully pastes them in the S & H green stamp book until it's filled. The more books she fills with stamps, the more stuff she can buy from the redemption store.

"The wheelbarrow with the rubber wheel will have to wait now," Louise tells him from the window. "Mama saw the sheets and wanted them."

"What the heck are you'uns saying to me?" Daddy squints like the light is too bright. "My head hurts."

Mama touches Daddy's hair and says, "Never mind. Here I am running at the mouth. The doctor thought you'd like a peaceful room to heal. You might even start feeling like writing songs again, Tom. Might be . . ." Her words fall away, but her eyes are filled with love. She covers Daddy with a quilt and says, "Rest, then we'll have supper together. You're home, Tom."

Then, Mathew the Mennonite waves good-bye and heads over to his truck.

"Mr. Mathew, thanks for carrying our daddy home."

Mathew the Mennonite nods. "I was glad to do it, Olivia."

I pick up Appelonia, and she crawls onto my shoulders. Louise takes Gentle and the twins inside with Grandma Horace. Becksie and Jitters race ahead, calling, "We'll help make supper!"

"He will be better soon and will want to thank you

himself," I say. "You're welcome to stay to supper. Daddy always said you were the finest carpenter this side of the Smokies. His memory will come back by and by . . . and hopefully, that radio will quit playing in his head, you reckon?"

"I do believe so," says Mathew the Mennonite, climbing into his truck, leaving us to get situated, but I want him to stay. He knew us before—like we used to be.

"By the way, I almost forgot to ask—how are your girls doing, Ruth and Sarah?" Appelonia drools on my arm, and I wipe it off.

"They're all right."

"Tell them they ought not to be such strangers. Are they readers? They might could come by the lending library truck and see what strikes their fancy."

Mathew the Mennonite nods. "They have a lot of chores, Olivia."

I get desperate, but I try to keep my voice calm and steady. "Us too! The chores don't stop, I swear. Hey, have you been keeping up with current events of the world, Mr. Mathew? We have to give a current-event report every week on a local, state, and national current event at school. Do you have any to suggest?"

Mathew the Mennonite pats my shoulder, but I shake him off.

"Mr. Mathew, could I ask you a question? Do you

think a girl can be about anything she desires? For instance, I am going to travel the world singing songs. When I tried to explain that in a report once at school, a bunch of kids said, 'Who do you think you are, traveling the world?' but I didn't care. Way I see it, we got one life and—"

"Olivia! Let the poor man go home to his family!" Grandma Horace snaps from the porch, so I back away.

"Bye now. Your girls sure are lucky to get to have school at home. Did you know our teacher made Rusty Frye lick Ivory soap last week for chewing gum? You ever been forced to lick soap?" I wipe away an irksome tear that sneaks its way out of my eye.

"It will just take time, Olivia."

"Shoot, I know that. I got dirt in my eye is all. You can go. I know you don't want to be hanging around here all your life."

He waits for a minute and starts the engine.

"Thanks again for helping, Mr. Mathew," I call as he drives off, but I am ashamed that I talked on and on. From across the two hollers, Samson, Mathew the Mennonite's peacock, screams a wail that boomerangs through the treetops. He always cries when he hears Mathew the Mennonite's truck coming home.

Then Caroline yells from the front porch, "I just saw

a fairy!" She grabs Cyrus, and they take off running together, but Gentle calls, "They're over here," and she dances under the red maple, twirling her arms in the air. Cyrus cries, "Maybe we'll find some Cherokee Little People, too! Hurry!"

Louise wanders back outside and flops down beside me. Uncle Hazard stretches out between us and lets me scratch his belly. "He's home," Louise whispers.

"If you can call it that." I dig my toes into the dirt.

"You got to give him time is all. Be patient."

I'm sick to high heaven of being patient. I've had months of being patient. I want him to be like he used to be. . . . Today was supposed to be that day. I lie back on the grass and spy the moon, the exact color of buttermilk glimmering across from the sun in broad daylight. "Louise, I'm sorry I bothered you about your smokehouse paintings."

My sister shrugs. "Never mind about it. Reckon you can't help shooting off your big mouth about everything." She laughs, and instead of getting mad, I laugh too.

I ask her, "Say, what are them shades of yellow again?"

"Saffron, butter, lemon, golden, canary, honey, goldenrod, amber, flaxen. Why?"

"Well, I got another idea for a song I wrote the other

day." I reach for my guitar, which is always nearby, and pluck out the chords to this new song. . . . It's funny, but if I have my guitar with me, I can just about stand anything.

Buttermilk Moon

I'd like to sip a buttermilk moon
And taste a lemon-cut sun.
I need yellow, sunny honey money days soon . . .
And nights of sweet canary stars . . .
Yes, I'd like to sip a buttermilk moon. . . .

I'll try to think of the next verse. I intend to sell my songs. I have to. Since that man in the smokehouse clearly won't be picking up a banjo anytime soon. . . . First chance I get, I'm going to have a peek inside the "Everything Box." I ain't sure, but I know that some-where in the house Daddy's got a file called "No Thank You Notes from Nashville." I figure Mama might keep it in the Everything Box, which we're not allowed to touch. She's got confidential matters in that box that I'd like to examine further.

As for other ways to earn a penny, we're just gon-na have to come up with a plan. Mama knit a heap of sweaters all winter, and my job at the bookmobile will

start up again come summer. We'll grow vegetables and
store them in the root cellar for the winter. Root cel-
lars are real good for keeping all sorts of foods fresh
like potatoes, onions, apples, and even the canned fruits
like peaches and blackberries. They also make fine hiding places, summer or winter, 'cause the temperature
always stays the same.

From far off, we hear the sound of a hunter's rifle
crack through the silent afternoon. It almost sounds like
slow firecrackers, leaving a sorrowful echo in the valley.
A swirl of young birds flies past us low to the ground,
stopping and starting up again. Wish I could go with
them. Louise may run as fast as a jackrabbit, but I sure
would like to fly. Seems like I almost could as I gaze up
toward Buck Mountain and Ghost Town in the Sky. I
send a telepathic message to my brother Emmett pretending to be just like Saturn Girl, his favorite, from
the planet Titan. *"Incoming message to Emmett Weems
at Ghost Town: Hear this, hear this. Your daddy has come
home, and he is not himself."*

*I'd like to sip a buttermilk moon
And taste a lemon-cut sun,
Lie in the middle of a golden afternoon,
Hiding away from everyone.
Yes, I'd like to sip a buttermilk moon. . . .*

CHAPTER FOUR

Turn Off the Radio!

MAMA SHOVES SOME red-lettered bills into the Everything Box, but it just makes some of the other papers inside spill out onto the floor. She picks those up and pushes them back inside, shutting the lid tight. Daddy used to keep his money in there, like a mini-bank. Now Grandma Horace keeps her check from Social Security in there before she mails it to her bank in Enka for deposit. Mama's money from her sweaters used to go in there too, but she hadn't sold any in a few months, what with Tom-Bill getting born and Daddy coming home. So the Everything Box is also like the family bank.

"Why can't I organize it for you, Mama? It's a mess."

"You keep out, Livy Two. I got important papers in there, and I don't need kids rummaging through it.

What do you want in there anyway?" Mama demands.

"Nothing, I just . . . nothing." I can't tell her about wanting to send my own songs to Nashville. Then she'd really hit the roof. She or Grandma Horace might burn up a letter addressed to me with a Nashville return address—drop it right in the woodstove. Although Mama wants Daddy writing songs, I think she's afraid for me to start down that "heartache path," as Grandma Horace calls it.

It's a curious thing Daddy being home, because it's like he's not home either. He's a different daddy living out there in the smokehouse. Mama says his doctor at the Rip Van Winkle rest home said it's just going to take time.

"How much time you think?" I ask her after supper one night.

"Livy Two, if I had the answer, don't you think I'd tell you? Now go pour out the dishwater into the garden, and don't spill it on the floor."

I dump the soapy water in a watering can to pour on the plants in the garden, since soapy water keeps the hornworms off the 'maters and the tater bugs off the 'taters. I stand in the middle of our garden, which is shaped like a giant circle—Daddy always liked a round garden with each plot of vegetables like a piece of garden pie. The crooked lady scarecrow is perched at the center, high above the corn like some spirit of the night in a straw hat and old cotton dress and a pair of cellophane fairy wings held together by wire hangers and tape. Caroline calls her "Stella, the fairy scarecrow."

I look toward the quiet smokehouse, where a light burns in the window. Grandma Horace has Gentle and the twins out there to say good night to Daddy. Through the window, I catch one of his old smiles when the little ones kiss him, but Caroline still keeps her distance. Daddy's wisp of a smile is just that, but it makes me feel like he's maybe in there somewhere. The new daddy has yet to touch his banjo, but at least he agrees to join us at supper and breakfast. Mama helps him eat sometimes because of the way his hand shakes, and she rubs his head with lavender when he gets his headaches. Standing there alone in the garden near the crooked lady scarecrow, I guess I can't help thinking that maybe he'll turn around and say, "Fooled you, didn't I? Get me my roasted peanuts! Got a song to write, and I need your help, Magnolia Blossom."

When Grandma Horace and the little ones leave the smokehouse, calling, "Good night," Daddy cries after them, "Don't go. I want a story. I got a headache."

Grandma Horace says, "Now hush, Tom. I need to get the little ones to bed. Livy Two or Jessie will be out in a minute to read to you."

I climb the red maple to get my E. E. Cummings book. I hope he likes the ones I read him tonight. Who can tell? The other night, I read to him, "who knows if the moon's a balloon," about a land where it's spring all the time and "flowers pick themselves." I saw me and Daddy sailing up high in a balloon moon, but when I finished reading it, he was already asleep. I tell my worries to Louise, only she's just glad to have him home and insists, "He's still Daddy."

The more I try to get used to him, the harder it is. He yells about the radio playing in his head and headaches, and he only wants to eat yellow food: cornbread, mush, cheese grits, golden potatoes, lemon pudding. He's real particular about it. I guess the biggest worry is how he took a walk the other day without telling nobody, and Mama had to send us to fetch him. He was only up by the baby waterfall that runs into the creek. He was picking up stones and putting them in his pocket. When I asked him if they were for Emmett's rock collection, he said, "I am missing my words. What's that over there?" He pointed to Gentle's tire swing.

"Called a tire swing, Daddy. A rope with a tire. You hung it up yourself last year with one of Grandma Horace's flat tires."

"Not me!" He shakes his head like some kid who knows everything.

"Yes you! I helped." I try not to snap at him, but he's so ornery. I read him Emmett's latest letter in my nicest voice.

Dear Livy Two,

Uncle Buddy has a new hoby now. He's still making birdhouses, but he's also making walking sticks and carving Bible quotes into the wood 'cause he says the Bible-thumpers are more willing to fork it over if Jesus is involved. Sory I can't make it home these days. I'm real busy being a gunslinger. Soon. Soon. Tell Daddy I said hello.

Love, your brother, Emmett

Daddy listens to the letter and when I'm done, he asks, "That it?" Then he goes back to picking up little stones.

While we're in school, Gentle watches Daddy with her ears, and calls for Mama or Grandma Horace when she hears him going off for a walk on his own. I can tell that Mama is worried because she can't keep an eye on him twenty-four hours a day. But since Louise hates school so much, Mama's been letting her stay home more than usual to help too. Grandma Horace doesn't like it, though, and warns that our sister will turn into some kind of "odd bird" if we don't put a stop to it.

And I guess our teacher, Mr. Pickle, feels the same way, because one afternoon, he stops me, Becksie, and Jitters after school and says, "I need to speak with all of you."

"Yes, Mr. Pickle." Becksie smiles. She's wearing her "Vote for Me" Maggie Queen pin, attempting to look very adult.

Mr. Pickle folds his arms across his chest and says, "How is your father?"

Becksie says, "Oh, much better. He gets stronger every day. He's been home a few weeks, and Mama and Grandma Horace say it's a miracle."

"I'm glad to hear it, but I'm interested in another miracle taking place—and that would be your sister Louisiana returning to school on a regular basis."

"Oh, that miracle." Jitters bites her lip, but Becksie jumps in all prim and proper. "Me and my Grandma Horace couldn't agree more, and I'll see to it myself."

"Please do," Mr. Pickle replies. "And you tell your mama that if your sister does not start coming to school every single day like the rest of you, then your family will experience what's called an official visit from the truant officer."

Jitters yelps, "Oh no, oh no, oh no! What's that?"

When Becksie says, "School police," Jitters drops all her school papers, and they go flying everywhere, so she and Becksie chase them.

I say, "Yes, sir, but Louise was truly sick with something that has a funny name."

Mr. Pickle says, "Was or is? And what would that something be this time?"

"She's just about kicked a severe case of pleurisy or something."

Becksie and Jitters stop and look at me like I've gone crazy, but I've impressed myself with all the afflictions I've invented for my sister to skip school: *bloody imbedded splinter, sparkling lights migraine headache, vicious dragon stomach flu, gangrene blisters, tore-up sprained ankle, a close encounter with a water moccasin.*

Mr. Pickle puts a hand in the air as if to block an invisible slingshot of lies. "Unless a child is at death's door, the child needs to be in school, and you may take that message home to your folks and to your sister. Now, I do appreciate all the creative calamities your sister seems to have experienced, Olivia, but Louise needs to regain her health by tomorrow and be at her desk ready to work, no excuses."

"Yes, sir." But I know only too well how such news will sit with my shy sister.

Mr. Pickle marches back into the school, and Becksie says, "My Lord, why can't we have a normal family? It's hard enough running for Maggie Queen and trying—" But she stops talking when she sees Evie Pepper, the most perfect girl in school, the girl most likely to win Maggie Queen, walk by with her court of ladies-in-waiting. Evie Pepper has silky golden hair and wears store-bought dresses all the way from Asheville, and even one from Raleigh. Why would a person go all the way to Raleigh for some old dress?

When she sees us, she stops and says, "Why hello, Becksie, Livy, and Jitters. How is your poor daddy doing, bless his heart?" Evie Pepper offers her most gracious smile, which makes me want to smack her a good one.

Jitters wails, "What if they send poor Louise to jail? Will we be able to visit?"

Naturally, this spikes up Evie Pepper's curiosity about ten notches, but butter wouldn't melt in that girl's mouth. "Is everything okay at your house? I'm sure our church could help. We're doing a clothing drive, and I'd like to help the less fortunate."

That does it. I'm so mad I could spit, but before this turns ugly, Becksie says, "Evie, thank you so much, but we couldn't be better! Honestly, thanks for asking, though. Bye!" She grabs me by the arm just as Pokey McPherson, our bus driver, blasts the horn from the mean yellow school bus. *Honk, honk!* "I ain't some Smoky Mountain chauffeur service. Come on or don't, but this ship is sailing."

As we board the bus, Rusty Frye crosses his eyes and

holds his nose, making his posse of runts laugh, but I ignore them. I sit with my sisters and cast my mind off to all the faraway lands I will visit when I can call my life my own, away from the Evie Peppers and Rusty Fryes of this world. Pokey pulls slowly out of the parking lot, but he floors it down Highway 19, because Pokey never drives slow when he can drive fast.

Jitters tugs on me like some nervous Nellie. "Are you going to tell Louise or should Becksie do it?"

Becksie gives me a serious look and says, "I believe, as the oldest girl, I should be the bearer of such bad news. Besides, they won't send Louise to jail for skipping school."

"They won't?" Jitters breathes a big sigh of relief as the mountains race by our window on the speeding bus.

"Nope, they'll send Mama or Grandma Horace instead," Becksie explains.

I cover my ears as Jitters really hits the roof.

Becksie hot-foots it to the garden to deliver Mr. Pickle's edict to Louise, who is planting a hill of summer squash. Her eyes fill with tears at the dire warning, but Grandma Horace, who wears her olive-green glass eye, which means no-nonsense, says, "I told you so. What did I tell you? Louisiana Weems, you are going to suck it up. Enough of this silly shyness. Mind over matter."

"I hate school. If I don't get this garden planted, how are we supposed to eat?" Louise digs the shovel in the ground harder, slapping tears away.

"You can plant after school and paint too," Mama calls from the front porch, taking in the whole drama. "We'll all pitch in, darling."

"But I was just about to plant more marigolds to keep the bugs out, and I wanted to go down to the farm store and buy some lacewings and ladybugs to eat the aphids. I can't just keep picking them off the leaves all the time. Soapy water's not near enough."

"Yeah." Cyrus holds up his fingers, smeared yellow from picking bugs off the plants. "See all the blood juice from the bugs?"

"Yuck!" Caroline frowns. "Bug juice."

Grandma Horace says, "School. Tomorrow. Get some gumption, young lady."

Louise says, "But Daddy needs me! Don't you, Daddy? He hates to be left alone."

Daddy stands on the front porch next to Uncle Hazard, who suns himself in a pool of late-afternoon light. Daddy says, "What is this place? Where did this dog come from?" Uncle Hazard snores, not a bit insulted by Daddy's questions. "My head aches."

Louise says, "Daddy, you brought him home to us from Knoxville last year. He comes from Hazard, Kentucky. You named him 'Uncle Hazard.'"

Daddy fires back, "Not me! I do not know that dog. Turn off the radio. Turn off Hank Williams! Tired of hearing other musicians making money and not me. . . ." He pulls his brown bathrobe tighter around him and swallows an aspirin for his headache without even drinking a drop of water.

Hank Williams is no doubt playing on the radio somewhere, but he sure isn't in our holler . . . only in Daddy's head. From inside the house, Gentle sings the words to "I'll Fly Away." *I'll fly away, oh darling, I'll fly away . . .*

And her singing makes me remember the very last night before the accident last year, back before everything changed. Daddy had come home late from his gig on the Cas Walker radio show, and I could hear him talking to Mama on the porch, and he said, "What did you let the kids fall asleep for? I missed them all day, Jessie."

Mama said, "Good Lord, Tom, I'm beat. I had to get them to sleep early, so I could get things done."

Daddy said, "Just let me go in and say good night to them."

"No, no, you'll get them all riled up. I know you. Now sit and—"

"I won't. I swear."

And before she could stop him, I could hear him come whistling down the hall to our big bedroom, where we were all asleep in our bunk beds, and when he opened the door and stood in the light from the hall, Cyrus yelled, "Daddy!" and we all jumped up out of bed to go hug on him. He grabbed up Gentle and Caroline, who nuzzled on his neck in their little nightgowns. Then he fried us all up a bunch of roasted peanuts on the front porch woodstove, and we played old songs like "Shady Grove," "Greenback Dollar," and "I'll Fly Away." Mama was mad at first, but Daddy nodded at me to keep playing, and he made Mama start dancing with him, and she started laughing, and I thought how that night I was the luckiest girl in the whole world to have a daddy like that. If I'd known the accident was going to change everything, I never would have let him out of my sight.

CHAPTER FIVE

Dandelion Sister

THE NEXT DAY, we wake up late and rush around like crazy on account of how Pokey McPherson will be screeching up to the bottom of the holler any minute, blowing his horn to beat the band. I yank on my jumper and try to find a pair of socks that will stay up. I hate how all of us girls have to wear dresses to school, but it's the law of the land. Mine's more wrinkled than usual since Caroline rolled around the garden in it yesterday, pretending first to be a chrysalis, then a butterfly.

At the breakfast table, Louise asks, "Mama, can't I pretty please stay home just one more day?" She wears one of Grandma Horace's dresses because she's out-grown all the girl-sized jumpers, and her heavy hair is all curls and knots, rising up in the warm spring air despite a severe brushing. "How about this?" Louise pleads. "I'll start reading the set of encyclopedias, be-ginning with *A*—I swear."

After the car wreck, the encyclopedia company that Daddy used to work for as a door-to-door salesman sent us a brand-new set of last year's 1962 encyclopedias along with a card that read, "Best wishes on a speedy recovery, Mr. Weems."

But Mama is not being fooled with the encyclopedia offer. "Louisiana Weems, don't fuss with me. My nerves are shattered with all I got to do. I want every last one of you in school. I don't need added troubles." Mama's face looks haggard, like she ain't slept much, as she nurses baby Tom-Bill and gives Appelonia a biscuit to gnaw on. She was up late arguing with Grandma Horace again about money and "the lack thereof!"

Becksie busts into the kitchen in a purple dress with daisies. It's a hand-me-down from the Methodist church, but she sewed daisies to the collar just in case some kid might recognize the cast-off dress. "Where's my lunch? Please no black-bean sandwiches. Can't we just for once buy bologna?"

Grandma Horace stalks into the room. "Bologna? What am I? Bank of Enka?"

"When I'm married, my icebox will be stocked with bologna," Becksie vows. "But right now, I'm late! I got five quart jars for pennies with my school picture taped on each one. Mama, could I please deliver them to stores after school? The person with the most pennies wins queen, and the money goes to help the school. Please?

Evie Pepper's so far ahead now, and I will not let that Miss Sweetness and Light win."

"That's right! No victory for Evie Pepper!" Jitters stomps into the kitchen, pulling up her socks, which bag around her ankles like worm sacs.

"Please, please, don't make me go to school," Louise whispers, raspberry splotches appearing on her cheeks. "I really don't feel good."

"Who's Miss Sweetness and Light?" Gentle eats her oatmeal. "She sounds nice."

"Can I deliver the penny jars, Mama?" Becksie pleads.

"Only if Livy Two goes with you and you'uns make it quick. I want Louise and Jitters home after school to help. Now hurry up and eat your breakfast."

I keep quiet, but the last thing on earth I want to do is deliver penny queen jars around Maggie Valley, campaigning for my bossy sister to win. I'd much rather sneak up to Ghost Town to visit Emmett or go fishing.

"When can we start school? We're big!" Caroline bangs her spoon on the table.

"Me too! And Cyrus!" Gentle says. "Let's us all go to school."

Cyrus drinks his buttermilk. "I want to go to Egypt to meet mummies, no school."

Grandma Horace stirs molasses into her coffee. "I

hear the bus. Hurry! And none of your foolishness, Louisiana Weems. March into school with your head held high!"

Grandma Horace's orders only make Louise slump farther down in her chair, dreading the day. We finish breakfast and step outside on the porch where the early-morning mist from the mountains clings to the air in pale wisps of smoke. Gentle says, "Smell the air . . . it's fairy-catching weather."

As we move off the porch, we almost trip over several sacks of clothes left on the steps with the note: "Hope this helps! God bless y'all. From a Filanthropist friend."

"What does that mean?" Jitters asks. "Fil-an-thro-pist."

"A do-gooder who can't spell worth a lick," I say. "That's sad." But I can practically see the steam pouring out of Becksie's ears. We know who it is . . . it has to be. I decide not to fuss about helping my sister deliver the penny jars after school to stores. That Evie Pepper has gone too far.

"What do you children know of this?" Mama's face flushes pink, because this "gift" smacks of a handout, something she hates worse than being poor. Daddy was the same way once, always yelling, "We're doing fine. I can feed and clothe my own kids."

Caroline says, "Maybe the mountain fairies brought it in the night, because they love us and—" but Cyrus interrupts her. "No, I bet it was the Cherokee Little People Mama told us stories about. They play tricks, but they can be nice too, right, Mama?"

Becksie groans in desperation and stomps off to the bus stop with Jitters.

Grandma Horace pats Mama's arm. "Leave it for now, Jessie." Thank the Lord she says it. Otherwise, we'd be dragging it with us on the bus to deliver to the folks who really need it. Grandma Horace hands me a sack of taters to give to the lunch ladies in order to pay back for the days we do eat in the lunchroom. It's a bartering system. Everyone on the bus knows when you can't pay 'cause they see the sack of taters or turnips for the lunch ladies, and sometimes we get called "Tater Girls."

We walk down to the end of the road to wait for the bus. "They're a bunch of Lilliputians," I tell Louise. "Never was a short boy who didn't see a tall girl as a target."

Becksie says, "That's right. You can't help being so tall. It's just a fact of life."

Jitters jumps back and forth over a puddle. "It's better than going to jail, Louise, which is what will happen to Mama and Grandma Horace if you don't go to school!" Jitters lands smack in the puddle and jumps back out again. "I'm wet."

The bus screeches to a stop, and we look toward the sunken face of Pokey McPherson. I point at Pokey. "Why, he looks like a jack-o'-lantern gone rotten."

Louise tries to laugh a feeble laugh, but her heart isn't in it. As Pokey McPherson pushes open the bus door with his lever and shouts, *"All aboard,"* the tiny criminals in the back press their faces against the window. Somebody yells, "Put on your gas masks. Weems in sight! Watch out for the giant one too! Now she's back!" I feel my face burn. Poor Louise. Do we really smell? Not Becksie, since she's mostly always clean, and Jitters is pretty neat, but it's hard to stay scrubbed and perfect in such a crowded house.

When I drag Louise on with me, I stop right by Pokey and tell him, "I want you to do something about those convicts-in-training in the back. They're bothering my sister."

Pokey spits a stream of brown tobacco juice into a cloudy Coca-Cola bottle. "I ain't Haywood County's sergeant of arms. They pay me to drive the bus. Now sit down."

I glance at the steering wheel and speedometer, wishing I could tell if he has that governor switched on or off. The governor is a device attached to the engine to make sure the bus driver travels at forty-five miles per hour, no more. But Pokey drives a lot faster than that, so I'm positive he fools with it.

"Oh, yeah?" I lean in close. "Maybe I will tell the authorities that you been messing with the governor, so you can haul down the roads at alarming rates of speed."

Louise nudges me in the back to quit it already.

Pokey McPherson's face starts working. "I never had no accident in my life. Why do you think they hired me to drive this here bus?"

"Maybe because nobody else wanted the job."

"Maybe because I'm a professional, you smart-aleck."

It's all too much for Louise, who can't hardly face the sight of one stranger, much less a whole busload, and Pokey's bottle of tobacco juice isn't helping. She jumps off the bus and throws up her oatmeal in a scrub of weeds. Rusty Frye shouts, "Boy-howdy, it's worse than ever! Wish we had a bomb shelter to protect us from Louisiana Weems!" The kids on the bus grumble with disgust. "Ewww! You see that?"

"What's the verdict?" Pokey McPherson guns the engine.

"Just go," I shout at him. I tell Becksie, "Take the taters and our book bags. We'll get them at school."

I hand them to her through the window. Becksie is too proud to show it bothers her to hold the taters, and Jitters just follows Becksie's lead.

Pokey yells, "Suit yourself." He gives me a dirty look and takes off down the road.

Bug-eyed Rusty shouts out the back window, "You can run, but you can't hide, Tater Girls! I seen you throw up . . . we all did!" His voice gets swallowed up in the dust and gravel.

When the bus is gone, Louise whispers, "Wish I was a dandelion or a dolphin swimming in the South Seas." She wipes her mouth with the back of her hand.

"Louise, I swear you can't let a bunch of pissant boys get your goat."

"Or maybe a whole field of wild dandelion flowers—a bright, honey-gold field. Or buttercups or poppies or bloodroots or hearts-a-bustin' flowers. Haven't you ever wanted to be something you're not?"

"Sure I have—like a world-famous explorer or astronaut or singer on the radio, but not a dang field of hearts-a-busting flowers. Come on!"

"I intend to memorize every bird, flower, fish, and color in the world."

"And I'll write songs about it all, but now, we got bigger fish to fry." I grab her arm. "Come on. Race ya! I'll be Saturn Girl, and you get to be the fearless

Lightning Lass. Let's cut down this way over toward Jonathan's Creek."

Louise thinks about my proposition and then says, "I'd rather be Invisible Kid—then I could go anywhere," and with that, she is gone in a flash. She runs like wild fire on those long legs. I chase after her.

Dandelion Sister

My sister wants to be a dandelion flower . . .
Or maybe a tulip or a rose.
My sister wants to hide in sweet white violets
And bloom in a field only she knows.
Dandelion Sister, don't cry . . .
Dandelion Sister, don't sigh . . .
Dandelion Sister, no lie . . .
One day we'll go off to seek our fortunes . . .
You and me, my dainty flower.
Paint your stories rich and bold . . .
So people stare for hours . . .
Dandelion sister, no lie . . .

CHAPTER SIX

Penny Jars

WHEN WE WALK in late, I practically got to drag
her to her desk. Me and Louise are in the same class,
because she's real smart at tests, so they bumped her up
to the sixth grade, but nobody believes she's smart on
account of how she likes to sit in the back by the window and keep to herself.

Mr. Pickle glares at the interruption. He's got himself a face that comes to a grumpy point, and he's forever sucking on ginger drops dipped in raw honey to
clear his sinuses. He claims they are agitated by chalk
dust and croupy children, who need to wash their hands
more often and cover their mouths when they cough or
sneeze and so forth. He goes to Miami Beach, Florida,
for vacation to escape.

"We missed the bus and had to run," I start to say,
but then Rusty Frye interrupts, "'Cause that big Tater

Girl barfed up her breakfast. Saw the whole thing."

Louise looks like she'd like to die right then and there, but Mr. Pickle isn't interested in more details and says, "Enough! All of you get to work on your spelling words. Olivia and Louisiana, be on time from now on." I give him the note about Louise's string of absences, and by a miracle, Grandma Horace's cautious penmanship seems to satisfy him for the time being.

Louise endures school all day but hides in the supply closet at lunch and recess, so she can draw in peace. After school, I walk her to the bus, where Evie Pepper tells a crowd of kids, "I think the Queen of Maggie School should represent goodness, charity, honor, and very ladylike manners, don't you?"

Jitters races up to the group and says, "Well, my sister collected thirty pennies, and that is thirty votes right there. Did you tell them, Becksie? I counted for her. Three times!"

Becksie snaps, "Be quiet, Jitters! Go home with Louise. Come on, Livy Two."

Jitters's mouth falls open, scalded by her loyalty being flung back in her face. But the other potential Maggie Queens look pleased to hear Jitters's information, which means they probably already collected a whole lot more than thirty penny votes, but they keep quiet and smile their secret smiles. Jitters blinks back her tears. She doesn't understand about the pennies being secret votes and how you're not supposed to broadcast the number of pennies to your competition—at least not until victory is sealed.

Jitters climbs onto the bus with Louise, and I jump up to get Louise's attention, but she's already got out her pad and is sketching on the bus. When she draws, she seals herself off from the world, same way I do, what with playing my guitar and writing my songs. I wave to Louise and Jitters as the mean yellow school bus pulls away, but Louise don't look up, and Jitters only waves forlornly.

Me and Becksie start our delivery of penny jars up and down Highway 19, and Mathew the Mennonite drives by and honks. His daughter Ruth waves to us from the front seat. I want to flag them down for a chat, but Becksie yanks me by the wrist and announces, "I already picked out where to go, and it has to be different businesses than Evie Pepper. I don't want our penny jars sitting there side by side."

"Great idea." I try to sound interested, but Becksie hears the fake note in my voice, and says, "Livy Two, I know you don't want to do this, and you think a queen contest is silly, so I can do it alone if I have to. . . . Don't worry about me."

"I said I would, Becksie, so come on!"

"Well, just be polite to folks and let me do the talking. Now does this look all right to you?" She holds the jar with her school picture and a little sign on the jar that says, REBECCA WEEMS! YOUR MAGGIE QUEEN! PENNY A VOTE. VOTE FOR REBECCA!

"It's fine. Let's hurry, okay?" My eyes fall on the Ice Cream Churn, our first stop. A big sculpture of a strawberry ice-cream cone beckons. "I'm starving."

"Well, forget it. We've got more important things to do than think about food." Becksie sighs in exasperation.

Just as we're about to go inside, one of Evie Pepper's servants strolls up to us from the candy store next door, chewing on a red licorice whip. She says, "I guess you and your sister think you're gonna win on account of your poor daddy's accident and how folks feel sorry for you. I bet I'm right and I think—"

"You sure are right!" I interrupt. "In fact, we want all of Maggie Valley to feel real bad for us and pile on the pennies! That's the plan, only instead of giving them to the school, we're gonna take the trillions of pennies and buy plane tickets to Paris, France!"

Becksie speaks in a voice as sharp as cut glass. "Would you excuse us?" As soon we get out of earshot, she says, "I told you to let me do the talking, Livy Two. Now I'm warning you to act sweet or go home."

"But she—"

"I mean it!"

"Fine, I'll be sweet, but I won't feel it."

We drop one jar off at the Ice Cream Churn, which is crowded with kids eating all kinds of ice cream. I try not to notice the sundaes and banana splits and chocolate malts getting sucked down, not to mention the soft drippy cones. I could faint I'm so hungry. We leave another penny jar at the filling station, a third at the Burger Box, where Becksie starts clogging as she sees a troupe of cloggers in click-clackity shoes ordering sweet iced tea and hamburgers. "Oh, I wish me and Jitters could clog with real cloggers instead of just in the front room." Becksie's feet move faster and faster with each turn as we walk down the road.

"Why can't you?"

"I'm the oldest. I can't just disappear like you do whenever I feel like it. Mama needs me." She quits dancing all of a sudden. "I might even apply for a summer job today. You got one at the bookmobile, Emmett's at Ghost Town. Maggie Valley gets packed with tourists come summer. This isn't just about being queen."

"You don't have to be such a martyr, Becksie."

My big sister marches off without a word, and I have to walk fast to keep up. Next, we drop off another penny jar at the Maggie Store, where the shelves are crowded with sacks of flour, sugar, and cornmeal, and cans of coffee and tea. Dried meats and fruits fill another shelf. I love the smell of the Maggie Store, which somehow makes a body feel less hungry, but Becksie isn't one to linger, so we go to the Pancake House.

All the folks at each business have been nice about letting Becksie leave her penny jar near the cash register where the customers will see it to make a donation, but when we go inside the Pancake House, we find that Evie Pepper's already beat us to the punch. Her quart-size jar with a pink ribbon is all shiny bright perched up on the counter near the toothpicks and mints. She also has a real pretty picture of herself taped on her penny jar, which says "Olan Mills" in the bottom corner, a fancy photography place from over in Asheville. In the picture, she's standing by a fake waterfall and her face has been lit into perfection like something out of *LIFE* magazine.

The lady at the Pancake House says to Becksie, "Do I spy another Maggie Queen in the running? Put your jar right on the counter, darling." Then the lady goes off to take another order of pancakes. Becksie puts the penny jar next to Evie Pepper's, but Becksie's school picture is not exactly flattering, especially compared to the flawless Evie Pepper. She looks rather stern as if she's saying to the photographer, "Hurry up and take it!" We stand there studying the penny jars side by side with Evie looking like a princess and Becksie looking like, well, Grandma Horace.

A pair of old ladies pay for their pancakes and get interested in the jars. Becksie and I slip behind a booth to see what they'll say.

One says, "Isn't that the Pepper girl? Law, she's a beauty. Who's the other?"

"I believe it's a Weems child—lives up in one of the back hollers on the road up to Cataloochee Ranch. Family rents."

"The one with the ailing daddy?"

"I believe so."

"Bless his heart."

"Bless his heart."

The ladies drop pennies in both jars.

Becksie's mouth is grim, but she heads over to the owner of the Pancake House and says, "Are you hiring for summer? I need a job."

In my dream that night, Patsy Cline sings "I Fall to Pieces" while Daddy shrinks down to the size of Cyrus. I take him and Cyrus both to the snake house at Soco Gardens, only the two of them are running around so fast, I can't catch them. Mama yells, "Watch them, Livy Two!" And I try, but they're so quick as they race, looking at the copperheads, rattlesnakes, and water moccasins. Then Daddy turns to me and says in a grown-up man voice, "You're not hitting that note right." "What note?" I ask. "Well if you don't know, I'm not going to tell you, Magnolia Blossom Baby!" But soon the sound of loud talking itches its way into my head, and I'm awake, and it's Becksie, arguing with the air, so I say, "Who are you talking to?"

Becksie hisses over Jitters's snoring, "Nobody! Just that I'll never win queen."

"Why do you want to win that stupid contest so bad?"

"Why do you want to sing? I just do, okay?" She yanks the covers over her head.

Louise's soothing voice comes out of the darkness. "Becksie, I'll paint a poster for you. If you think it might help. For your campaign."

Silence.

Becksie sits up in bed. "You will? A good one, Louise? A real good one?"

Louise says, "I'll try."

Becksie turns to me and says, "Thank you . . . and Livy Two? I need you to do something too."

"Now what?"

"Write a song for me."

"I already delivered all those durned penny jars with you. Isn't that enough?"

"You write songs for everybody. The least you could

58

do is write one about me being the best queen the school is likely to ever get! Is that too much to ask?"

I flop down in the bed, ears jammed with Becksie's orders. I will myself to go back to the dream with Daddy to find out what note I was singing wrong, but I only see rows and rows of "Vote for Becksie" penny jars. I think of Daddy and how he won't be back to normal until he's up, running around, salting up his roasted peanuts, playing his banjo, swinging us through the air, kissing on Mama, ducking from Grandma Horace's sharp tongue, doing all the things he used to do. Then a song for Becksie actually does find its way into my head, but it won't be one I'll be singing for her anytime soon. If she don't win queen, I hope at least the lady at the Pancake House gives her a job. She and Becksie had a real good talk today. Of course, I could have added a warning or three to enlighten the Pancake House lady during Becksie's interview, but I kept my mouth shut. I try to hear Becksie's song in my head.

Becksie's Lament

I intend to be queen for Daddy.
Jitters, get my jewels, gowns, hairbrush, perfume—and
    hurry up too!
But black-bean sandwiches . . . Why must I eat black-
    bean sandwiches?

I intend to be queen for Mama.

Jitters, get my jewels, gowns, hairbrush, perfume—and
  hurry up too!

Bologna, please . . . Normal, please . . . Don't embarrass
  me, please.

For I intend to be queen. . . .

I will be queen. . . . Please?

CHAPTER SEVEN

Enka-Stinka Savings & Loan

ON SATURDAY MORNING, Mama pours bird-seed into the feeder. So now we've got all sorts of birds that hang around our holler, from grackles to hummingbirds to cardinals to indigo buntings, Mama's favorite. She has started feeding the birds more regular ever since Uncle Buddy sent down a birdhouse he built as a "Welcome Home/Get Well Quick Now" present for Daddy. It's a funny sort of present, but it got Mama talking to us about birds and how much she loved them as a girl. Even Grandma Horace seems happy to see the birds flitting around the birdhouse, which is actually two houses attached together. One side says "His" and the other says "Hers" and the sides are connected by a bridge of glued acorns.

I keep an eye on Appelonia, who scoots all around the garden on her bottom in her diaper. We can always tell where Appelonia has been 'cause she's a scooter baby, not a crawler. All sorts of interesting items accumulate in her diaper, such as radishes, snap beans, and little maple seeds. Caroline collects the maple seeds that don't wind up in the diaper, because they favor baby fairy wings, but Cyrus says they're more like tiny helicopters, and he wings them spinning through the air. I pick Appelonia up, and she shrieks at the birds gathering around the birdhouse, clapping her hands. After a few Appelonia squeals, Daddy yells from the smokehouse, "Turn off that radio!"

"It's not playing. It's your ears hallucinating again!" I yell back at him.

"I hear Kitty Wells, by God!"

I don't answer. Instead, I kiss Appelonia's baby neck and breath in her soft curls. It's sweet to have babies around to kiss on when you got a sick daddy in the smokehouse.

While we're working on our big sister's campaign to win Queen of Maggie School, we read to Daddy, talk to him, play songs for him. He half listens, but I don't know what the other half does. It's like he wanders off someplace in his head right there in the thick of us. He cries easy and won't touch the banjo to save his life. Whenever I ask him if he wants to play, he says, "What for?" Gentle even takes his hand and runs his fingers over her Braille pages that she's just starting to learn to read herself. "Feel it, Daddy, one dot A, two dots longways B, C two dots sideways. . . ."

I read a book about Louis Braille to Gentle and the twins, the man who invented the Braille alphabet and who was blinded by an awl when he was little, and it makes me wonder what an awl looks like. . . . I know it's a tool for punching leather, but that's all I know. I also read a Helen Keller book. She was blind and deaf but spoke six languages and traveled the world, giving lectures with her teacher, Annie Sullivan. I read extra loud for Daddy to hear too.

"Gentle, listen . . . Helen Keller says right here that, 'Life is either a daring adventure or nothing.' What do you think about that?"

"I like adventures." Gentle ties bits of yarn in her hair and lets the strings drape over her eyelashes and lips. "Look at my face!" Gentle says. "I got rag-doll hair."

Daddy yawns. "What flavor is that car over there?"

"Flavor? The car don't have a flavor, Daddy. It's a brown station wagon."

"Brown! That's what I meant. Brown."

"But brown's a color, not a flavor."

"How about that."

"I was trying to talk to you about Helen Keller."

"Who?"

Gentle giggles, but I don't. It's not funny. If Daddy doesn't get serious about getting better, what kind of grand adventure will he have in store? I'm afraid to think. I get sick of trying to get through to him, but Louise takes him by the hand and leads him to the garden where he likes to sit and watch her work. His brown bathrobe fans around him like a sad royal cloak. I wish he'd put on regular clothes, but he prefers the bathrobe. Louise hands Daddy a container of lacewings and says, "Open it, Daddy!"

He pries open the lid and soon the garden fills with lacewings, gossamer creatures of emerald, flitting over the plants. Caroline skips along the edges of the garden, like a giant lacewing herself. "It's like you let a bunch of fairies loose, Daddy."

"What happened to me?" Daddy asks nobody.

"You had a car wreck, but maybe you'll get better." Caroline hops on one foot.

An official-looking letter arrives from our landlady in Clyde, a woman I call "Madame Cherry Hat," because she wears a hat with clusters of fake cherries around the brim. Makes my stomach jumpy to look at the cherries either in person or on her stationery. Mama and Grandma Horace exchange more heated words behind closed doors. It comes to a head one night down on the front porch when they think we're fast asleep, but I do not sleep when critical eavesdropping needs doing. I steal out of my window into the red maple, but as I get settled in the branches to listen to the snapping words on the porch, Gentle crawls out behind me. I whisper for her to go back, but she crawls out anyway, her hands feeling for a steady hold on the branch, before I pull her into my lap.

"Did you hear something?" Grandma Horace looks toward the woods.

"The children are asleep, Mama. So is Tom."

"Don't you miss next-door neighbors, Jessie? At all?"

"No, ma'am, I do not."

"Well, I have always appreciated next-door neighbors. What's wrong with being able to borrow a cup of sugar or exchange a kind word or two at the mailbox?"

Mama's knitting needles *click-clack* below us in the darkness. She's got a new sweater started to add to the heap of sweaters she knitted all the time she was pregnant with baby Tom-Bill. For the first time since I can remember, Mama is not pregnant, and I'm glad. I love babies, but we got more kids than we can shake a stick at.

"It's a peculiar thing about Emmett's paycheck. He sent it for a while and now it's all but dried up,"

Grandma Horace says. "Except for a meager ten now and again."

I freeze when I hear this because I have not breathed a word of Uncle Buddy pilfering Emmett's wages to pay his poker debts. Nothing Emmett hates worse than a blabbermouth sister.

"I'm sure Emmett has expenses up there," Mama says, "but I don't like it either. A promise is a promise, and Lord knows I taught my boy to keep his promises."

Grandma Horace says, "I don't think it's all on Emmett, if the truth be told. It's just a hunch, but my brother was known to take what he needed and then some."

Mama sighs. "Surely, Uncle Buddy couldn't be such a lowdown skinflint crook as to steal from a boy."

"He bears watching is all I'm saying." Grandma Horace strokes the mole on her chin, which is a sign she's been doing some serious thinking. "At any rate, the landlady letter was a wake-up call. I am not the Enka Savings and Loan. . . . Well?"

"Well what?" An edge creeps into Mama's voice.

"I have a plan, Jessie, and it's a good one if I say so myself."

Gentle starts to ask a question, but I shush her. If we're caught spying, we won't never hear the end of it. Thank goodness, the crickets and tree frogs have already begun a spring orchestra down by the creek.

Mama knits faster and says, "I know your plan, and I'm not moving this family to Enka. I didn't spend the fall and winter knitting sweaters and waiting for my husband to wake up so we could move back to the city with you."

Grandma Horace snorts, "I would hardly call Enka 'the city,' but it may come to that. We've been very fortunate that I've been able to rent out my family home to Mr. Shelnutt and his wife, Charlotte, but how long am I expected to finance this family and its tragic tale of sorrow? You might could even get a job yourself at American Enka as a secretary or at Champion Paper in Canton. The children could go to school in Enka, and Emmett could come home and get serious about his future. If he doesn't, that boy will wind up one of those carnival folk—a 'carny' is the word, I believe. One in the family is enough, thank you very much. If he were my boy, I would have—"

"He's not your boy, Mama. And he'll come home when he's ready."

Grandma Horace lets loose a long, woe-is-me sigh. "I seriously doubt that. My brother has made it a way of life—carnival shows, bad teeth, and living from hand to mouth. . . . Far as I can tell, your son is headed down the same path."

Mama's voice changes to a softer tone. "Did you see

what Louise did in the smokehouse? I've never seen such paintings. I want her to go to someplace and study art. Wouldn't that be something?"

"You had the chance to do the same—you painted all those birds for the school art show."

"Not those birds again. I do remember. . . . Purple finches, Carolina chickadees."

"Well, I still have them in Enka. But you couldn't be bothered after you took up with Tom Weems!" From the window, Louise gasps, and I turn around to see her listening too. I figure we're about to be caught spying for sure, but Grandma Horace is too fired-up mad to notice a thing. "And now you let your children run wild—it's the truth."

"What should I do? Give them each a toy and force them to sit still while I scrub the house clean? That was my childhood. 'Don't move.' 'Be still.'"

"Dredging up the past after all I've done for this family. Now listen to me. . . ."

Then Mama says something I have never heard in a lifetime of eavesdropping on grown-ups' conversations. "Mother, I've listened to you all my life, growing up in that American Enka house supplied by the plant, the smell of rayon and rubber from all those textiles in my nose every day of my childhood, so Daddy could walk to work. I swore when I got old enough I would move into the real mountains and make my home, not raise my kids next to a factory. Tom loved the mountains too. And we vowed we wouldn't have just one lonesome kid with nobody to talk to or play with. We wanted to raise a big family who could play music and dance, paint pictures and tell stories. I'm trying to do that. It's what we both wanted."

"Love and air may come cheap, but nothing else does."

Mama says, "Smell that honeysuckle? I saw a gray fox last week, and a flock of guineas found their way to right here in the front yard. I can think here. Tom is getting stronger every day. The mountains are what's going to get him strong again."

"I have mighty serious reservations about that statement. And you might consider Gentle too. She's going to need a special school. I think we ought to write to the Governor Morehead School for the Blind in Raleigh. I hear they take children young as five. You don't want that beautiful child to wind up uneducated. She's smart as a whip. I'm trying to learn that Braille card alphabet, but she's catching on quicker than me."

Gentle shakes her head and buries it in my chest. I stroke her back. No way am I going to let Gentle leave us, I don't care what Grandma Horace has up her sleeve. She can come to school with us. We'll make them let her into the Maggie School.

"Mama, don't think I don't appreciate everything you're doing."

"Jessie, I miss my neighbors. I miss my friends in Hominy Valley."

"I'm so tired, Mama. Please let me be awhile. I'll figure something out."

There is a long silence on the porch below of creaking rockers, the porch swing, and the clicking of knitting needles. Finally, Grandma Horace says, "Well, you better figure it out fast. And while you're doing it, I got another thing to say. So long as I'm the breadwinner and my musician son-in-law is finding his wits in the smokehouse, then this family is going to start going to the Peachtree Methodist church right here in Maggie. Every last one of you! My heathen grandchildren can get a regular taste of the Lord so long as I'm footing the bill. Beginning tomorrow morning, as tomorrow is Sunday."

Louise whispers, "Law, she don't quit, does she?"

"Not while she's got a pulse," I whisper back.

It's getting chilly, but we don't dare move for risk of being caught. Finally, Mama and Grandma Horace go into the house, and I crawl into the window with Gentle. Once we get under the covers, Gentle whispers, "I don't want to leave here, Livy Two."

"Course not. I won't let her take you off to Raleigh. Not on your life, Gentle."

"Promise?"

"I promise," I whisper as Gentle snuggles down between me and Louise, but I ain't sleepy yet. A pain inside me knows that Gentle may not be able to attend the Maggie School, but I don't want to think about that now. I pick up my guitar off the shelf above my bed and pick the chords to the start of a song festering in my head.

Enka-Stinka Savings & Loan

Grandma Horace is a lady,
Grandma Horace is a Methodist,
But Grandma Horace is not . . . the Enka-Stinka
  Savings & Loan.
Grandma Horace is a teacher,
Grandma Horace is a traveler,
But Grandma Horace is not . . . the Enka-Stinka
  Savings & Loan.
Do not ask for a handout,
Do not ask for a nickel,
Do not ask for a freebie,
'Cause . . . Grandma Horace is not . . . the Enka-Stinka
  Savings & Loan. . . .

CHAPTER EIGHT

The Everything Box

THE NEXT MORNING, buttery rays of morning sun shine through the window and hit the cubbyholes built into the far wall that hold our clothes. Mathew the Mennonite carved them, since the old-time chiffarobe fell apart from the damp. Louise painted each kid's name by their own cubby in pretty letters. Mama says the cubbyholes are a hope and prayer for order in this house, except they're a real mess right now, with clothes spilling out of each and every one. We're all supposed to keep our own cubby neat, but everyone forgets. On top of the cubbies sit three stacks of Mama's sweaters and some baby blankets and scarves too. She just needs to get to Waynesville or Asheville to start selling them. She finished the last one just before baby Tom-Bill was born over at the Haywood County Hospital in Clyde.

I wake with a plan. If Grandma Horace is going to

make everyone go to the Methodist church today, it's my one chance to get my hands on the Everything Box. I need to send my songs to Nashville, to the same place Daddy sent his. I know it's a long shot selling my songs, but last year, I won an Honorable Mention and check for twenty-five dollars at the Mountain Dance and Folk Music Festival over in Asheville—all because Daddy made me enter when I was too scared to try. So each and every day that I don't at least try, I feel like life is slipping by at breakneck speed.

While everyone gets ready, I huddle under the blankets until the moment of reckoning when Grandma Horace marches into the room. "Every-one's spruced up and in the car—even the babies. Now you're truly sick and not pulling my leg?" "I'm truly sick." I make my voice scratchy. "Hurts to swallow, my head aches."

"All right, you sleep. But come next Sunday, neither floods, famine, nor locusts are going to keep you from getting a dose of the Lord."

"Yes, ma'am. Bye. Say a prayer for me."

From my bed, I listen to Mama instructing Uncle Hazard to keep an eye on things, and he barks a bark that says he's up to the task and flops down on the front porch to stand guard.

So Grandma Horace hauls everybody off to the

Peachtree Methodist church, true as her word. Even Daddy, and I hear her get him into the car, saying, "If anyone needs prayers, it's you, Tom Weems!"

The second they're gone, I leap out of bed and drag a chair to the shelf where the Everything Box sits in the same place it always has. It's about a foot tall and about that wide and heavier than I thought. I lift it down and take it into the front room and hold it on my lap. My hands are shaking I'm so excited. The box is made of tin with a painting on the front of the White House and rose gardens under a turquoise sky. All I need is the "No Thank You" folder, and my tape from the Mountain Dance and Folk Music Festival, and I'll leave the rest alone.

I finger the latch—a little metal latch that isn't locked. When I open it, I see past-due bills, coupons, report cards, birth certificates, church bulletins, school newsletters, programs from some of Daddy's shows in past years, another envelope with Madame Cherry Hat's address in Clyde marked URGENT, scraps of recipes, check stubs, hospital papers, a few articles on rubella—the Germans measles that caused Gentle's blindness—from Dr. Addie Johnson, Gentle's eye doctor. I don't see how Mama fit so much stuff into one box, but she is real organized about everything. All the items in the box are divided by thick rubber bands.

One envelope says CASH & PAYCHECKS, but there's just a few dollars in it.

Then I find them just like I knew I would. Both things. "Livy Two's Singing Tape." And "No Thank You Letters from Nashville." I sift through the letters, and most seem to come from a man named Mr. George Flowers. They're all pretty much the same form letter that begins "Dear Musician," but on the last letter, he has scribbled, "This one was close, Mr. Weems. Keep trying!" It is a sign, sure as anything. So I copy down the address of Mr. George Flowers and go to close the box, but I find one of Daddy's new songs. I can tell it's new because of the way it's scrawled on the back of a paper bag in pencil. Daddy always typed up his lyrics after he wrote them out longhand. The song is called "Mountain Mint." I can't read it very well, but I'll show it to Daddy to see if he remembers it.

I know I should hurry up and put everything back, but I can't help it. I just want to keep searching through everything. I find a stack of black-and-white photographs from the old days. For years, Mama has meant to get photo albums or true scrapbooks, but she hasn't got around to it yet, and we don't have that many pictures anyway, since our camera broke, and we haven't replaced it. I find an old postcard that says *1952 Greetings from Louisiana*" from Daddy to Mama that reads:

*Dear Jessie darling, I miss you something awful. How
are the three little ones? We're playing at every honky-tonk
from Bossier City to Baton Rouge. Trees grow right out of
the bayou here. Saw sunrise and thought of you. Let's name
the next one after this state. Sure is pretty. Love, Tom*

So that's how Louise got her name. I never even
knew Daddy played on the road in Louisiana with a
band. I can't wait to show my sister. Next, I sift through
the pile of photographs that go all the way back to Tur-
key Creek, where Mama and Daddy courted, but then I
find a picture I ain't seen before, and I can't take my eyes
off it as I cradle it in my hands.

It's like there's three parts to it. In one part of the
picture is Daddy, bending down on one knee with his
arm around Emmett as a little boy. Emmett is grinning
big at the camera with his little-boy hands folded together resting on Daddy's hand. Emmett's blond curls
whirl up pretty on his head, and he wears little black
socks and tiny black-and-white saddle shoes. (Even
during the years when Grandma Horace wouldn't
have a thing to do with us, she always sent us boxes of
new saddle shoes every year, rain or shine, speaking or
not speaking . . . usually not, but those boxes of saddle
shoes came all the same.)

Daddy has a cowboy hat hanging off his arm, and

his coal-black hair is combed so fancy perfect the way he always fixed it right before a gig. He wears a scarf looped around his neck tied to the side—jaunty-like and sporting. He knows by a mile how handsome he is at the very moment the flash goes off, hugging on his happy boy. Behind Daddy in the background is Mama, wearing a print dress of butterflies, one of the babies on her hip, but their heads are cut off so it's hard to tell which one. Jitters, maybe? I'm there, too, off to the side in a chair, one leg tucked under the other, a jump rope looped around my shoulders, while Becksie sits behind me, legs draped over the side. We got on saddle shoes too. I'm smiling, but Becksie looks stern just like she did in her school picture. Her hair is long and curly, but mine is cut short above my ears.

Then all at once, I start crying like I can't stop. It's a gush of tears that won't quit no matter what. I hug my knees hard to my chest and bury my head and cry hard, silent tears. I wish I had a secret magic power that would allow me to step back into old black-and-white photographs and whisper warnings into the ears of those smiling faces. *Avoid the road completely on August 13, 1962, and all will be well. Don't catch the German measles in the spring of 1959, and you'll get yourself a healthy baby with strong, seeing eyes.* More than anything, I wish I could show this photograph to Daddy this very minute,

stick it in front of his face and say, "Come back to us like
you were. See this here? Please, Daddy."

I close my eyes and whisper, *"My daddy, Tom Weems,
is the finest, handsomest man ever to pick up a banjo and
roam the hollers and hills of North Carolina."*

I dry my tears but vow to carry Daddy's photograph
with me every place I go until the daddy out there in
the smokehouse smiles at me again like the daddy in
the picture. The late-morning sun slants through thick
cobwebs hanging in the top corner of the window. I put
his handwritten song, "Mountain Mint," in my pocket.
I'll type it up as soon as I get the chance. Then I put
everything else back as I found it, so Mama will be none
the wiser. I only keep the tape, the song, the postcard of
Louisiana, and Daddy's picture. I hide everything in my
secret box in the red maple inside my E. E. Cummings
book and put the sheet of tin back over the box. But I
keep Daddy's picture next to my heart.

More than an hour later, the sound of Grandma's station wagon grinds back into the holler. Uncle Hazard
races up to the car to greet them, barking his fool head
off. I'm out by the woodpile chopping wood for the fire.
It feels good to chop wood, hearing the piercing crack
as it splits in half. I like the steady rhythm and the ache
in my arms. I swing the ax down hard on the stump, so

they can all see how strong I am, but they don't notice. I wave to the family as they get out. "I'm better. How was church?"

But everyone climbs out of the station wagon looking glum, and Grandma Horace marches into the house without a word.

Gentle hears me chopping wood and heads my way, tapping her cane. She asks, "Can me and Caroline take some wood scraps and make a fairy house?"

"Sure, take what you want." I give her some pieces of wood, and right away she starts figuring out their lengths for the fairy houses.

"Don't get splinters. What happened at church?" I ask her, but Caroline answers, "The radio in Daddy's head was real loud. Grandma Horace got mad as the dickens."

Cyrus says, "He told the preacher man to turn it off."

"But only he heard the radio, nobody else did," Gentle says.

Jitters consoles Becksie and says, "Maybe Evie Pepper didn't notice!"

"Oh, she noticed all right." Becksie paces up and down, wringing her hands.

Louise shakes her head. "Everybody was staring and staring and staring."

Mama says, "Well, the music was real pretty, wasn't it, Tom?"

Daddy doesn't answer, but he follows Mama up the steps and sits down on the rocking chair. Mama gives him a kiss on the head before she goes inside with baby Tom-Bill, but he just he rocks back and forth, watching me chop wood.

"Daddy," I ask him, "you want your banjo?" I feel the picture of him burning a hole in my pocket. It might could be a magic picture containing miracles, but Daddy's eyes flash with rage. "No banjo! Quit asking me that." He gets off the porch and walks his funny, tippy walk to the smokehouse, banging the door shut behind him.

Stung, I blink away tears. Why does he have to be so dang grouchy? Without thinking or looking, I grab the next piece of wood to split it in two, only to find myself face-to-face with a copperhead snake, who raises its ugly head and opens its mouth wide, waiting, eyes coal black and fixed on me. Uncle Hazard snarls at the creature as if to say, "Come on! Take me on!" I can't even breathe I'm so scared; a low buzzing roars like thunder inside my ears. The copperhead don't make a rattle like a rattlesnake, but he's trying to make up his mind to do something—his mouth is a venomous hole with a skinny red tongue hanging out. I feel like the Tin Man from *The Wizard of Oz* froze up solid. I know I should back up or run, but my knees lock up, and I'm so scared he'll bite me or Gentle and Caroline, who are just a few feet away, oblivious to the danger.

"Let's leave food for the fairies," Gentle says.

"Every night. What do they eat?" Caroline asks.

"Shut up, don't move! Copperhead!" I whispered in a strangled voice, and I can feel the little girls hush to see what's wrong, but I'm afraid to move. Could a copperhead bite more than one person? I try to swallow the cry in my throat, but it's bone dry. From out of nowhere, Louise looms up behind the snake with a hoe and strikes it across the head. She beats it—*whack*—but the copperhead loops itself up and around the hoe like a twisted rope until Louise gives the hoe one last tremendous smash, and the snake falls to the ground. Black-and-orange bands wind around his body up to his head, which is a dark copper color. Grandma Horace comes out on the front porch and takes one look at the mangled snake on the ground and cries, "Lord have mercy, everybody all right?"

"Yes, ma'am," Louise says. "I reckon so, except for him." She points the hoe at the snake.

Mama rushes out on the porch with Tom-Bill in her arms. "What happened?"

"See for yourself. Snake." Grandma Horace sits down

on the rocking chair. "Good thing Louise is shy around folks, and not snakes."

Mama says, "Well, thank goodness. I can't take another—"

"Mama, the beans are burning!" Becksie shouts from inside the house, and Mama flies back in without finishing her thought.

Grandma Horace says, "And to think I used to spend my Sunday afternoons in Enka, napping, reading the newspaper, none the wiser, snake-free."

Cyrus says, "Did we almost die of snakebite?"

"What's it look like?" Gentle wants to know.

Caroline stares openmouthed at the snake on the ground before she says, "Like the biggest snake in the world, and Louise killed it."

Gentle says, "Can I touch it?"

Louise says, "Sure, honey," and she takes Gentle's hand and lets her run her fingers along the dead snake's back, but Caroline shrinks back, screaming, "I'm not touching it!"

My knees feel like jelly as I sit on the stump and stare at the dead snake. I have no desire to touch that thing. I try to breathe right, but my heart is a jackhammer in my chest.

"You okay?" Louise sees my hands shaking.

"Thank you," is all I can manage to say to her.

"Maybe you'll check the woodpile first, Livy Two," she adds with a smile.

Caroline asks, "Well, I'm glad that old snake didn't mess up my pretty dress. Say, Grandma Horace, are we gonna go back to that church again?"

"Every Sunday like clockwork, long as I have anything to say about it," she says. "Now, one of you children make yourself useful and fetch Grandma Horace a cool drink of water, so I can sit out here on this old porch and take in the scenery." She takes out her cobalt-blue glass eye, polishes it on her apron, and pops it back in her eye socket.

Louise says, "Well, I reckon I'll go work on Becksie's Maggie Queen poster since the excitement is over." She takes her paints and brushes and paper and heads up to the back field to paint in peace. I don't feel like chopping any more wood, so I go inside and get Grandma Horace a drink of water. The springwater from the backyard runs right through the hose directly into our kitchen sink. I fill up her glass to the brim.

CHAPTER NINE

Maggie Queen

A FEW DAYS before final voting for the Maggie Queen Contest, me and Louise arrive at school hot and sweaty from running. It feels great to run the two miles instead of facing Pokey McPherson and his mean yellow school bus. Me and Louise could run day and night up and down those hills, summer or winter. She's faster than me, but whenever we get separated, she whistles one of her ear-splitting whistles, and I can find her in a second. When we're running fast, it almost feels like we can fly, and it makes me stop thinking of Daddy and all of it. I had a real flying dream the other night where I flew over Maggie Valley above the coves, hollers, and balds of the Plott Balsams, Setzer, and Dirty Britches Mountain too.

We race to the classroom to see who gets there first, and Louise wins as usual. Mr. Pickle glares at our noise even though we arrive before the bell. Mr. Pickle is what's called a teaching principal, because while he's still learning the ranks of being a principal, he's also a teacher.

"Well, well, well," Mr. Pickle sniffs, popping a ginger drop into his mouth. "Louisiana Weems. All these weeks in a row of coming to school. On time too! I know our dear classroom is a giant petri dish swimming with all kinds of evil bacteria, but it is a tremendous relief to see that you're not bedridden with such calamities as sparkling migraine headaches, dragon flu, and close encounters with water moccasins."

Louise gives me a smoldering glare that translates: "What lies did you say about me?" I avert my eyes. I'd clean forgotten to mention all the creative catastrophes I'd bestowed upon her, so I change the subject. "Mr. Pickle, we couldn't dare miss today. Our sister Becksie is in the homestretch of campaigning to be the Maggie School Queen. Did she give you the poster that Louise made? We didn't want to run with it and make it all sweaty. You're gonna love it!"

Mr. Pickle says, "Yes, she did, but I—"

Before he can say anything else, the bell rings just as Rusty Frye snorts, "Poster or not, it won't do a lick of good, telling you right now. Evie Pepper is winning, and my money is on my big brother, Jake, to win king.

I've collected a ton of pennies from my daddy's lumber shop to help Jake."

Mr. Pickle says, "Take your seats, students. And Rusty Frye, that's all very illuminating, but you may also sit down." He turns his attention to Louise. "I'm glad, at any rate, that my words had some effect on you and your family, Louisiana, and that you've made up your mind to join us on a regular basis. How is your daddy?"

Louise ducks her head and whispers, "All right," in the softest voice.

Billy O'Connor pipes up. "That's not what I heard. My ma says he might be retarded and y'all need help. I am supposed to ask what you need. That's what she said, because Evie Pepper told her the whole sad story at the Plott Grill." I freeze, and it takes everything in me not to march back there and have a hard swing at him this very second.

"My daddy is not retarded." I force the sob out of my throat. "He's on the mend. You can tell that to your know-nothing flap-jaw ma! Maybe you're the retarded one."

Billy stands up and knocks over a chair. "Take that back, ugly girl!"

"Make me!"

"This will cease this very minute!" Mr. Pickle warns in a low voice.

"I'm sorry, but I'm not taking a thing back!"

Louise sinks down low in her desk like she's never laid eyes on me before. Mr. Pickle drags me out into the corridor and starts the lecture. "Olivia Weems, if I see that kind of behavior again, I will contact your mother or your grandmother myself. Clear?"

A gaggle of sweet-faced first-graders, without a care in the whole world, march by holding hands on their way to square-dancing practice in the gym for the spring show. A few stare outright at me in fear, and I'm ashamed to be cast as the troublemaker kid in their eyes, but Billy O'Connor had no right. The first-graders stare a bit longer before they stop and get interested in a poster of who else, but Miss Evie Pepper, with all the trimmings: "Cast your pennies for me! Your Mountain Maggie Queen! Vote for me!"

Something snaky in my heart makes me itch to draw a hairy mustache on that perfect face, but Mr. Pickle interrupts my thoughts. "Now, Olivia, I know your family is facing uncertain challenges at the moment, but I am raising young ladies and gentlemen to grow up to become responsible citizens and contributors to the world." He points to a painting of John F. Kennedy on the wall. "Our president would say the very same."

"I'm sorry, but it was a matter of honor."

"Honor or no honor, you will apologize to Billy O'Connor."

"Yes, sir." I hang my head and slip back into the classroom to my desk. I look at Billy, who is blowing bubbles with his spit and trying to pop each one with his pencil. "Sorry," I hiss at him in the fastest, quickest "sorry" ever uttered in the whole universe.

"You can keep your old sorry." Billy pops another spit bubble.

"Fine, I will keep it," I whisper back. "And I hope you enjoy your future home at the Brushy Mountain State Penitentiary."

Later, when lunchtime rolls around, I can't find Louise, so I go check the classroom supply closet.

"Go away!" she orders when I knock my special knock so she'll know it's me.

I yank open the door. "Louise, folks are gonna think you have serious mental problems, carrying on this way."

She's sitting on the floor, hugging her knees close to her. "Bald-faced lies. And why'd you yell at Billy O'Connor? Why make it worse? You're just like Grandma Horace setting up there on your high horse, judging the whole wide world."

"Take that back. I'm nothing like her."

"You are too. You got a big mouth. Now leave me alone."

"You can choke on the crayons and erasers in there for all I care!" I slam the door until it rattles. *Bam!* How could she say those things to me when all I've done is try to defend her and our family? Well, I'm done. She can fight her own battles. I head to the lunchroom to trade the taters for a week's worth of lunch tickets for me and my sisters. I also clean the lunch tables after all the kids are done eating in exchange for free banana popsicles and homemade rolls. The cafeteria ladies make the best rolls. Seems like I'm always hungry no matter what. When the tables are wiped clean of crumbs and kid stickiness, I get my rolls and stuff them in my mouth, but my throat's crowded with sadness. That durned old Louise. How dare she say that? I am not a thing like Grandma Horace! I brush away a stupid tear. No way am I going to show her that postcard of "Greetings from Louisiana" and how she got her name—not while she's being so lowdown hateful.

For the whole rest of the day, I keep away from Louise, and she steers clear of me too. Before dismissal, Mr. Pickle says, "I have an announcement. May I have your attention, please? All eyes up here, for I would like to show you something very special." Then he carefully picks up Louise's poster, unrolls it, and studies it for a long time. He can't quit looking at it. Finally, he says, "This is beautiful, Louisiana. You have a rare and wonderful talent."

"Let's see, let's see!" The kids in the class crane to get a good look, but Mr. Pickle isn't finished. "I've been keeping track of this new arts school that's just been established in our state. I wonder if it might not be right for you? The North Carolina School for the Arts is what it's going to be called. Now, it doesn't open until 1965, two years from now, over in Durham, but it's something for you to think about for high school."

I don't look up, but a chill spikes my blood. First, Emmett runs off to Ghost Town, and lately, there's been that talk of Gentle going off to Raleigh to some blind school . . . and now Louise and this Durham place to some art school? Our family feels like it's on the verge of splintering . . . and what about me? What if I'm the one left behind while everybody else goes off on adventures? Maybe I ought to run off to Nashville on a Trailways bus and seek my fortune—not say a thing about it to a single soul.

Mr. Pickle turns the painting around and shows it to the class. A silence falls over the room, but it's an awed and respectful silence, and though I'm still mad at Louise, I got to admit the picture is a beauty. Louise has painted Becksie standing up on Fire Rock at Ghost Town in the Sky on Buck Mountain. Fire Rock is where the Cherokees would send messages through smoke signals across the valley in the olden days. Becksie is dressed like a mountain girl, but her message is delivered like an Indian girl's could have been from atop Fire Rock. In the painting of the smoke swirling above Fire Rock, it says, "Rebecca Weems—Queen of the Maggie School" with Becksie gazing across the valley at Soco Gap in the full dawn of morning, while beautiful Cherokee children dance on the other side of the mountain.

For once in their sad, puny lives, Rusty Frye and Billy O'Connor got nothing to say. The other kids in the class all crowd around Louise's picture. She puts her head on the desk as if she'd like to disappear for good. After school, Mr. Pickle hangs the poster in the auditorium so that all the kids can see Louise's masterpiece for themselves.

When we get home that day, there's another letter from Emmett.

Amish Country
Late May Something 1963

Dear Livy Two,
School out yet? Uncle Buddy should be paying me back any day, but I'm sending you another ten dollars to give

to Mama. Guess where I am now? Amish country! The blacksmith of Ghost Town let me drive with him up to Amish country in Ohio to buy the old-fashund stagecoach. He's a real nice man, and his wife looks like Saturn Girl's twin sister. Her name is Clare Whelan. How's Daddy? Tell him . . . I don't know what . . . tell him hey.

Love, Emmett

P.S. I read about how this Russian cosmonaut lady is gonna go into orbit in June. Her name is Valentina Tereshkova. First lady in space. I cut out the picture. Her nickname is "Seagull." Heck, maybe you'll be second.

Very funny, Emmett, family deserter. . . . You can go all the way to Amish country in Ohio, but you can't come home to visit Daddy? And I'm down here doing your jobs, chopping wood, fighting off copperheads, and whatnot? I almost wish I had been bit, a tiny bite—one that didn't hurt but would have forced me to take to my bed like Beth from *Little Women*. I'd have recovered but not until Emmett had come home to plead for forgiveness over the poor, battered body of his snakebit sister.

I should just go on up to Ghost Town and haul him back by the scruff of his sorry neck, but I been too busy with chores and fighting with Louise and composing (in my head) the letter to Mr. George Flowers, the

Nashville music man. Does Nashville offer record deals to twelve-year-olds? Should I lie about my age?

Louise and I don't talk about the fight, but we are careful with each other like we're as breakable as fine-lady china teacups or something. In fact, lately my heart feels like a teacup filled up with burning hot tea that could spill over and shatter at any second. I'm used to Becksie's harsh words, but not Louise's. I need Louise to love me no matter how stupid I act, but I can't tell her that—it'd be like I was sniffing around for sympathy, and I'm not, by God, I'm not. I also keep hoping and searching for the light to break through in Daddy's eyes and really look at us again like he sees us and knows us and is glad to be home. I walk with him up and down the holler, all of us do, with Uncle Hazard trotting along beside us. Mama says Daddy needs the exercise, but we don't talk about important things like we used to in the old days. I might say, "Watch out for the rock," and he might say, "What rock?" I point and say, "That rock." And we just keep walking, but going nowhere. I help him steer clear of stinging weeds on the path.

I guess Louise must be missing the old Daddy too, because one night I catch her in the smokehouse showing him flashcards. "What's this letter, Daddy? Say it," she says.

He looks hard at the picture of the apple and the *A*, but doesn't say a word.

"I know you know it," she says. "Quit pretending that you don't, and I mean it."

Daddy blinks and looks harder at the picture and then he says, "Apple pie."

"Close enough!" Louise hugs him. "Close enough."

And later, when she crawls into bed with me, I say, "I saw you in the smokehouse with him. Where'd you get those flashcards?"

She yawns. "In spite of what certain people think, sometimes, hiding in a supply closet at school isn't the worst idea in the world. But they're not very good. I may have to paint him some flashcards myself."

"He'd like that, I bet. . . . Louise? I'm sorry." But she doesn't answer, so I turn over in bed, careful not to touch her. I look out the window at the stars, which makes me think of Livy One, my oldest sister who died at birth, and my namesake. I used to talk to her all the time and tell her my secrets, but it seems like I think of her less and less now. What's the matter with me? Maybe she's forgotten us too. I panic and send a part telepathic Saturn Girl message/part prayer to her up there in the ring of Seven Sisters stars, Pleiades, like the seven sisters in our family. *Dear Livy One . . . Sorry I've not talked to you in so long. Please fill our house with love instead of misunderstandings and misspoke words. Make Daddy better . . . like he was. Could you answer for once? Please?*

The good news is that during the last week of school, the donation jar beneath Louise's poster gets filled with more pennies for our sister, Rebecca Weems, the Maggie School Queen hopeful. Evie Pepper's poster may be pretty, but it's nowhere near what Louise has created. On the last day of school, which is a half day, we are called into the auditorium to hear the announcement. We stand to say the Pledge of Allegiance and recite a poem called "Memories of the Sugarlands" by Alie Newman Maples.

Mr. Pickle says, "Now, boys and girls, the big moment has arrived. I have the results for our new Queen and King of Maggie School. Rebecca Weems has won queen by a margin of six pennies and Jake Frye has won king by a hundred pennies. They will be our new eighth-grade king and queen beginning this fall for the whole year." There is a big whoop and Becksie looks like she might actually float into the air. But Miss Sweetness and Light Evie looks like she swallowed a lemon.

Mr. Pickle says, "I encourage all students to be good sports and good citizens of our mountain home and offer your congratulations to both Rebecca and Jake. And all who participated and contributed should be proud. You've raised one hundred sixty-four dollars and fifty-three cents for our school, which means we're closer to putting blacktop down for our basketball court."

Rusty Frye does a dance and yells, "Told you so! My brother is king!"

Evie Pepper sulks, and her court soon clucks around her in sympathy. Becksie looks so flushed and radiant with happiness standing next to Louise's painting. Jitters races up to her and falls into her arms. "Whoops! Sorry. Congratulations, Becksie!"

Becksie hugs Jitters, but moves over to Jake Frye, who smiles at her, and somebody takes their picture. For the first time in my recollection, Becksie looks real pretty, in her Maggie crown, wearing a garland of azaleas and sweet white violets. I feel someone standing behind me. Louise whispers, "Thank the Lord she won."

"I'll say, or we'd never hear the end of it. It's one of your very best, Louise."

"Thank you, Livy Two." And like that, we're not mad anymore.

It's our summer vacation, and I am mighty relieved to be done with mountain royalty contests. I intend to get back to my summer job with Miss Attickson at the bookmobile and check out some books on brain trauma. Louise's borrowed set of flashcards is already helping Daddy, but we got a lot of work to do to bring him back to us like before. As we clear out our desks for the summer, Mr. Pickle says, "Louise, I'd like to see you a moment."

She approaches his desk like a deer in headlights, but he only has a book for her. He says, "This is an art book by an artist named Vincent van Gogh. He was from over in Holland, and he had a lot of brothers and sisters just like you. I'd like you to take it home this summer and have a look through it and tell me what you think."

Louise nods and hugs the book to herself and whispers, "Thank you."

"Olivia?" He calls me over to his desk too. "I understand you're working for Miss Attickson this summer at the bookmobile. Now, don't give her any trouble. She works hard to get books around the mountains. As for me, I'm off to Miami Beach as usual."

"Have fun. And Mr. Pickle? Miss Attickson is my good friend. I would never give her a minute's trouble."

The bell rings and we are free for the summer. We fly out to catch the bus, and Louise reads her book all the way home. When Rusty Frye tries to insult her with, "Hey, beanstalk, hope you don't grow another foot," my painting sister is far off in Holland with Vincent van Gogh. She shows me a picture called

Potato Eaters and whispers, "It's like us getting called 'Tater Girls.'"

As Pokey McPherson speeds past the Soco Gardens snake house, he gets word of the Maggie Queen and King election and offers Becksie a surly, "Congratulations, kid!"

When the bus drops us off at home, Becksie shouts to the house, "Hey, where is everybody! Guess what? I won queen. I'm queen of the school! Come out and congratulate me."

Grandma Horace calls from the front porch, "Well, don't let it go to your head, Your Majesty. Right now, we've got a missing daddy to locate." It's almost lunchtime, and it turns out that Daddy took off hours earlier, and Grandma Horace is fit to be tied. Mama's gone out in the station wagon hunting him.

CHAPTER TEN

Hello, Little Mennonite Girl

WHEN THE BIG black telephone blasts its jarring *r-r-r-r-r-r-ring*, we're already gathered around it, waiting, but Grandma Horace says, "Nobody touch it. I am the one answering the telephone today." She picks it up and says in her most dignified voice, "Hello. This is Zilpah Horace. I am the mother of Jessie Weems." *Zilpah.* What a funny name, and I realize I've never before known Grandma Horace's first name. *Zilpah. Howdy, Zilpah.* . . . I don't dare call her that to her face. She's always been Grandma Horace, not Granny or Meemaw or Nana.

The person on the phone turns out to be the lady from the Pancake House, who asks to speak to Mama. Grandma Horace holds the receiver close and says, "She is not here at present, may I take a message? Where? He ordered what? In his pajamas and bathrobe? All right, we'll fetch him as soon as my daughter returns with my station wagon. Thank you very much." She hangs up the phone, turns to us, and says, "Your daddy is down at the Pancake House eating blackberry pancakes and bacon and sausage and grits. If that don't beat all. And he's wearing that brown bathrobe, probably looking like one of Jesus' Apostles himself."

"How's he gonna pay for it?" Becksie asks.

"Yeah, how?" Jitters demands. "'Cause I think we're flat broke."

"That is the sixty-four-million-dollar question." Grandma Horace's lips purse together in a knot.

Not a minute later, Mama peels the station wagon into the holler, spitting gravel, and yells, a sob in her voice, "Any word? Or sighting? I've looked everywhere."

Grandma Horace calls, "He's fine, Jessie. Catch your breath, daughter. Apparently, he walked out to the road and hitched a ride. Mercy me."

Becksie yells, "Mama, I won the Queen of Maggie School. I won queen!"

But Mama's already got the car in reverse, backing down the road. I race up to the car and say, "Let me go too, please?" Before she can answer, I jump into the front seat and she hits the gas to the Pancake House, burning rubber all the way. Daddy isn't the only one who likes to drive fast in the family.

When we walk inside the cool air-conditioned Pancake House, Daddy is about halfway through a second order of mountain blackberry pancakes. He smiles when he sees us and says, "Well, hello there!"

The waitress wears a name tag, VAL, and smiles at Mama. "Your husband sure likes his pancakes."

Mama puts on her polite, company face and says in a tight voice, "Thank you." She turns to me and says, "Livy Two, sit with Daddy. I need to speak to the manager." I suspect she's going to apologize and see about a rain check for Daddy's breakfast. But as she finds the manager over by the counter, I watch her take out one of her knitted baby blankets from her handbag to show it to her, and I overhear the manager say, "This isn't necessary, Mrs. Weems. We're just glad your husband is feeling well enough to come down here to the Pancake House and have his breakfast. He did a real nice job at Settlers Days last year, volunteering to select the talent, playing that claw hammer banjo."

The face of that manager glows with kindness, and I'm so glad she wasn't mean to Mama, what with Daddy ordering up the moon without a penny in his brown bathrobe. The relief on Mama's face is evident, and I look over at Daddy, who says to me, "Hungry?" He pushes his plate toward me, and I take a bite of his mountain blackberry pancakes swimming in maple syrup. Pure heaven on earth.

When I take a second bite, he says, "Give it back now."

"Okay, Daddy." I push his plate of pancakes back toward him, and he keeps eating like a house on fire. Mama leaves Val a fifty-cent tip for her trouble. I know she'd leave more if she could.

When me and Mama arrive home with Daddy, all the kids race out to the car to greet us. Daddy gets settled on the porch and lets Cyrus wrap up one of his arms like a mummy. Gentle and Caroline flutter around him in their fairy wings, wanting to know how he liked his pancakes.

Daddy says, "They were some all-right pancakes swimming in blackberries."

Caroline is getting more comfortable around Daddy, mostly because it seems like Daddy enjoys being around the little ones best. Us big kids seem to bewilder him, but the little ones play and don't want anything from him other than that he's nearby.

Before Grandma Horace can put in her two cents about "the entire fiasco," Mama turns to Becksie and says, "I'm proud of you winning queen. And right before we left the Pancake House, the manager asked me if you still wanted to have that summer job you were asking her about the day you dropped off the penny jar. You'll work the Saturday and Sunday morning shift as a waitress. The lady who runs the place is as sweet as she can be. You'll wash dishes on the other days if you want. I said you did."

Becksie says, "Do I get to wear a uniform with an apron?"

"You sure do. It's in the car. And your first shift will pay for Daddy's breakfast. We don't take handouts."

Becksie says, "I'm going to be a real, true working girl. I won queen and got a job all on the same day! I'll keep my wages in the Everything Box, just like Daddy did."

"Heck, I wish I could get me a job at the Pancake House too!" says Jitters, kicking at the dirt.

A kind and benevolent expression spreads across Becksie's face. "When you're all grown up like me, Jitters, I'll put in a good word." It's almost too much to stomach. But what can we say? The queen has spoken, and maybe we'll get some free pancakes out of the deal.

That night Mama makes a list. She aims to get each of us older kids some kind of employment for the summer to keep Grandma Horace from banging the Enka-Stinka drum of doom, which beats louder by the day. Becksie is now set at the Pancake House, Emmett is somewhat gainfully employed at Ghost Town, and I start the bookmobile with Miss Attickson in a few days. The Everything Box will start getting regular deposits again for the bank, but what about Louise's contribution? That's what I'd like to ask, but I don't, even though I do have excellent ideas on the subject. Sometimes, my head aches from money this and money that. . . . I wonder if other kids my age got to worry about money the way I do? I bet that old Evie Pepper is planning for a sandy summer at Myrtle Beach. It's hard not to feel low-down-scraping-the-ground-petty-jealous when I look at what other folks got and what we don't.

Still, if we all work, we might bring in enough to scrape by, so long as Mama can start selling her sweaters again like she did last year. Mama has a way of smiling at folks and getting them to see they need sweaters for the winter even on a hot summer day when it seems winter will never come. She's decided to name them "Jessie's Mountain Sweaters." But first, she's got to get Daddy more situated here at home. No more lighting off to Lord knows where again, and so she puts her plan into action by calling upon the services of Mathew the Mennonite.

On the first full day of summer vacation, I come back from fishing with Uncle Hazard to the sound of hammering and pounding. Mathew the Mennonite's truck is here, and he's in the smokehouse fixing up some shelves. His daughter Ruth is in there helping him, hammering away. This is the first time he's brought her along, so I guess she's real good at carpentering too. When she catches me looking at her through the open window, she waves and I wave back, and I go find Louise to tell her about Ruth. Louise is out in the garden watering the pie plant, so Grandma Horace can make some summer pies come August. Pie plant's official name is rhubarb, but since it makes the best pies ever, folks call it pie plant instead.

"Cyrus," Mama yells, "chase those awful crows out of the garden lickety-split!"

"Yes, ma'am!" Cyrus grabs Caroline and Gentle, and they yell and scream at the black crows to beat it right now. Uncle Hazard joins them, barking away. He considers it his sacred duty to chase off crows and other varmints. Gentle goes over to Stella, our crooked lady scarecrow in the middle of the corn, and shakes the pole, which makes the lady scarecrow wobble and bow from her perch in her fairy wings. Gentle calls, "Woooooo! Woooooo!" like a midget ghost scaring off the evil black crows that fly off in all directions, flap-flapping and caw-caw-cawing. Rusty Frye says his brother, Jake, uses a .22 rifle to shoot crows right out of their garden. He likes to brag about how Jake is the best shot in Haywood County, and how his brother creeps out of the house with his gun at his side, so the crows don't see it and then *bam!* Mama won't have a .22 in the house, but it sounds like it does the trick better than the pie pans that hang off Stella—even if such information is coming from the likes of old Rusty Frye.

More loud pounding comes from the smokehouse. Will Mathew the Mennonite's efforts be the bait that makes Daddy want to stick closer to the holler? Mama flat-out refuses to put a lock on the door, which Grandma Horace highly recommended. Mama says the smokehouse is not a jail and she's no warden. Instead of a lock, Mathew the Mennonite is building a fine writing table (plywood and two-by-fours for now), and Mama has bought a secondhand typewriter from the rummage sale at the Peachtree Methodist Church for a dollar. She believes it will remind Daddy of the songs he needs to get back to writing. I want to ask her how she thinks he's going to write any songs when he still seems confused by flashcards and life in general, but today is not the day for questions—not from the way Mama stalks around the holler with her mad face, draping more strings of pie pans off the crooked lady scarecrow and then turning the crank for the laundry tub with a stony-hearted fretfulness.

I only wish I'd stayed fishing. When I'm fishing, my mind is clear, blank, with room for songs to enter, thoughts to ramble, and places to visit. But back here, there's always something that needs doing. Sometimes, I wish I could be like Triplicate Girl from the planet Cargg and be able to divide into identical selves to get all the work done around here. That'd be much more useful than Louise's wish to be Invisible Kid. I sure miss Emmett talking about all the superheroes. I dump the trout in a bucket in the springhouse, which is like an outdoor refrigerator, to keep them ice-cold for supper. I cross the yard where Caroline, Cyrus, and Gentle race past me to sit on the bench, followed by Jitters, who tails them like she's directing traffic. Since Becksie is at the Pancake House, Jitters has been promoted to babysitter, and she means to involve Daddy in the games whether he wants to or not. She acts like the train conductor and grabs a stick to wave around and blows her whistle.

"All aboard, you orphans!" Jitters cries. *"Clang! Clang!* That's the final warning bell. Aren't you poor little orphans lucky to be going to a real home with other children like your poor orphan selves? Train to Orphanville is leaving soon." Jitters blows the whistle too hard, and it pops out of her mouth. Appelonia is scooting on her bottom around the orphan game, and scoots right over Jitters's whistle, which ends up in her diaper. Jitters fishes it out and says, "Yuck! My whistle's ruined by a baby diaper."

The little ones giggle, and Appelonia scoots up to Daddy, who stares down at her.

Uncle Hazard howls, *Barrooo!* in protest and slinks off into his pinecone palace. Jitters cries, "Get back here, orphan!" but he races off to freedom.

Daddy yawns and says, "I'm hungry. Time to get off the orphan train. Bye now."

Grandma Horace calls from the window, "Tom, don't you dare leave this holler. Come on inside and wash up. Lunch is almost ready."

Daddy gets up and walks into the house. The little ones jump up and follow him inside, much to Jitters's fuming. "Y'all just jumped off a moving train, I hope you know."

As they stomp off, I find Louise out staking the to-matoes in the garden, which are about the size of hard green apples now. She's also started painting a series of flashcards for Daddy, and she's using her van Gogh book to give her ideas. They're spread out on the ground to dry—flashcards of biscuits, molasses, honey, a banjo.

"Louise, Mathew the Mennonite's brought his girl here. Ruth," I tell her.

"I seen her already." Louise shrugs.

"Did you hide from her and not say hello as usual?"

She don't reply, so I know the answer. "Ruth might be nice, for all you know. Say, these flashcards sure are pretty."

"Thanks." Louise stakes up another tomato vine.

"Louise, I got something important to ask you. Now before you say no, remember that it's just a way of making money."

"What is?" She looks wary, pouring a bucket of water on the pumpkin plants.

"I was thinking that you and me could go to the general store in Waynesville on a Saturday and set up a booth outside on the sidewalk."

"A booth of what?"

"Portraits. You can draw portraits for two dollars each."

"Of who?"

"What do you mean of who? The folks who want them. There'll be lots of folks in town on Saturday doing their shopping and so forth."

"No. Besides, what about your job at the bookmobile?"

"On Saturdays, Miss Attickson goes over to Jackson County. Please?"

"Nope, no thanks."

"Why not?" I kneel down to help out weeding the radishes and beets. "We could ask Mama to come and sell her sweaters, too, like we done last year in Gatlinburg."

"I'm not going all the way over to Waynesville to draw pictures of strangers. What if they don't even like them? What if they hate them?"

"Louise, listen . . . we need every penny now or you can bet Grandma Horace will have us enrolled at the Enka-Stinka school before you can blink. Now, you don't have to talk, just draw. That's your great talent. Please? Come on, what's wrong?"

Her eyes fixed on the ground, Louise says, "I'm a freak, Livy Two. They're going to line up and laugh at me. 'Come see the giraffe girl in the Smoky Mountains! Louisiana Weems. Biggest gal—and then some.' I could join the freak show with those two-headed twins and the bearded lady and the pinheads and . . . and . . ."

"Louise, five-foot-nine is not freak-show material. They wouldn't hire you! Besides, what's more important, whether we find a way to make money and stay together or whether a few ignorant folks look at you funny?"

"But how can you be almost a year older than me, but I'm a foot taller than you? It's not natural." Louise weeds around the butter beans, jerking up the weeds as if they were the heads of all the short boys who'd ever tormented her.

I let her catch her breath before I say, "So will you go draw portraits of folks in Waynesville for two dollars a pop or not? We could get us a chocolate pie at Whitman's Bakery after. Or peach cobbler. Or an éclair. Please?"

A tiny voice speaks up behind me. "Say, you think I could come too?"

Me and Louise both whirl around to see Ruth standing over us, wearing her bonnet and apron like a true old-fashioned girl, with a sweet, shy smile on her face. In fact, she looks like Mary Ingalls from the Little House books with her sky-blue dress. I wish I could dress up Caroline and Cyrus and Gentle like little Mennonite kids. They'd be so sweet looking. She's a tiny thing, the opposite of Louise. My sister blushes but doesn't say a word, so I say, "Why do you want to come with us to Waynesville, Ruth?"

"'Cause I'm eleven like her even though I'm short and she's tall. And I'm an artist, too, only I build things, and that one there paints things." She points at Louise, who blushes even more, but Ruth says, "I didn't mean to listen to your talk, but Father talks about you all so much. So I'd like to come with you if he says it's all right."

"Say something, Louise." I give her a nudge.

But Louise's lips are sealed, eyes on the ground. Mathew the Mennonite calls out, "Ruth, I need you! Ruth!" from the smokehouse.

Ruth says, "I got to go." She turns to leave, but she stops and says, "Sometimes, I wish I could live at your place. It sounds exciting every single minute of the day."

It's funny how she calls Mathew the Mennonite "Father." It sounds so proper.

At that moment, Grandma Horace shrieks, "Cyrus, get that unsanitary salamander off the table if you don't want to see the sparks fly, young man!"

Ruth's eyes grow big, and nobody says a word, but then Louise laughs out loud, which is something she never does around strangers. I love the way Louise laughs, because it's hard not to laugh with her. She has this deep belly laugh, and it takes a while to quit once she gets going. Me and Ruth join in the laughter too.

Hello, Little Mennonite Girl

Hello, little Mennonite girl.
Well, hello, little Mennonite girl.
What are you doing, little Mennonite girl?
You can swing a hammer, you can wear your bonnet.
Hello, little Mennonite girl.
Nice to meet you, little Mennonite girl.
So nice to meet you, little Mennonite girl.
You can make a sister laugh, you can call a 'daddy'
   Father.
Hello, little Mennonite girl. . . .

CHAPTER ELEVEN

Dear Mr. George Flowers

THAT NIGHT AFTER everyone is fast asleep, I sneak into the smokehouse to write my letter to Mr. George Flowers, the Nashville music man, on the secondhand typewriter. Daddy's sound asleep, too, though my typing is loud. He looks like his old normal self when he's asleep. Good thing he sleeps heavy, because it takes me forever to type. I'm flat-out the world's worst typist. I bite my lip and keep typing, letter by letter, real slow, so as not to make a mistake. When I do make one, I just go back over it with an "xxxx" and start again. I got quite a few xxxxxxxxxxxxxxxs and xxxxs in the letter. I like Daddy's new song "Mountain Mint," which I took from the Everything Box a while back. It took near a month to figure it out, but I finally deciphered his hen scratch. I don't make a single mistake typing up "Mountain Mint." I will mail it all tomorrow on the job with Miss Attickson.

When I finish, Daddy's eyes are open and he's watching me, his face alert and curious.

"Daddy, you're awake. You want to hear my letter to Mr. George Flowers?"

"Who?"

"George Flowers. He is the Nashville music man who told you not to give up on your songwriting. Want me to read it?" *No answer.* "Well, like it or not, I'm going to read it to you. I'm putting one of your songs in there too. I'm also sending him the tape from the festival where I sang. I hate to send away our one copy, but it's the only way, since you're not up to auditioning yet. Remember how you made me sing that night in Asheville last year?"

"Nope."

"Well, listen up anyway and give me your candid opinion."

June 16, 1963
Dear Mr. George Flowers,

I am the daughter of Tom Weems xxxxxxxxx and I believe you know my daddy's songs because he sent you some banjo tunes from time to time in the past. You wrote to him a "Keep it up" note on your last form letter. I know that songwriters have to go through plenty xxxxxxxxxxx of rejection before they can sell a hit song and get famous, so I wanted to thank you for encouraging my daddy.

And I do not mean to sound full of myself, but as Tom Weems's daughter, I'm a pretty good xxx songwriter myself, and so I'm sending you some of my songs. It's a reel-to-reel tape of me singing them at the Asheville Mountain Dance and Folk Music Festival that Daddy made me sing at last year, and I'm sure glad he did 'cause I won twenty-five dollars and a tape too. These are the titles of my songs xxxxxxxxxxx:

Daddy's Roasted Peanuts
Mama's Biscuits
Grandma's Glass Eye
Floating Checks
Colors
Olivia Hyatt Weems
A Ring of Seven Sisters
Daddy

Daddy is recovering from a car xxxxxxxxx accident. However, he will be on the mend in no time and sending you more songs. In fact, I'm taking the liberty of sending you one he wrote before the accident called "Mountain Mint." But it would be best if you sent your reply care of Miss Attickson, my employer xxxx and friend.

Miss Attickson
Haywood County Bookmobile
Waynesville, N.C.

Sincerely,
Livy Two Weems
P.S. Here is "Mountain Mint," Daddy's latest.

MOUNTAIN MINT
By Tom Weems

When I wake up in the morning to greet another day, I
    taste that
good, sweet mountain mint. . . .
Oh, spearmint, peppermint, horsemint, and crème de
    menthe . . .
That's right, that dear mountain mint!
When I walk along the holler back in the piney woods,
    I smell
that fine, rich mountain mint. . . .
Oh, spearmint, peppermint, horsemint, and crème de
    menthe . . .
That's right, that dear mountain mint!
When I gather up my children to give their heads a
    scrub, I get a
whiff of pure mountain mint. . . .

Oh, spearmint, peppermint, horsemint, and crème de
   menthe . . .
That's right, that dear mountain mint!
When I grab my wife to kiss on her and squeeze her real
   tight, I
breathe in the finest mountain mint. . . .
Oh, spearmint, peppermint, horsemint, and crème de
   menthe . . .
That's right, she's my sweetest mountain mint!

"What do you think of my letter and your song, Daddy?
It's funny how I write songs so much like you. See how
your style has influenced me? And I've put your song to
music—want to hear me play?"

"No! No, ma'am! Who painted all these pictures?"
He stares at the walls.

I take a breath to keep my temper. "Louise did. Every single one."

"What happened to me?"

"You had a car wreck, a long time ago. Do you remember writing 'Mountain Mint'?"

"Not me. I didn't write that."

"Yes, you did! Make yourself remember, would you?"

"About what?"

"What year is it, for instance?"

But he doesn't answer. He only studies the red maple

painting on the wall, the deep roots painted all the way to the floor stretching up into a tree on the wall to the ceiling. "What's that called?" He points to a rainbow.

"A rainbow, Daddy."

"A rainbow," he repeats. "I am still missing my words."

"I know, but they're coming back a little."

"Where am I?"

"The smokehouse in Gentle's Holler. You named our place 'Gentle's Holler.'"

"No fooling?"

"No fooling, Daddy."

But he squints his eyes at Louise's Seven Sisters constellation in the sky above the tree, the brightest star being Livy One. I open the window wider. "You smell that honeysuckle? It'll be apples and woodsmoke come fall."

Slowly, he turns his eyes to look at me, and I pull up a stool by the bed. Daddy closes his eyes like a little kid who don't want to be bothered. I pick my guitar up and play a few notes of his song, "Mountain Mint." I'm just guessing on the tune, but the chord progression feels right in the key of G. With my hands on the neck of a guitar and Daddy right beside me, I can near about pretend nothing ever happened. He watches me move my fingers across the strings, but his eyes are sad. Maybe he's scared his playing is lost, but it can't be. He taught me how to play everything from chords to the slide to all of it. A pounding commences on the smokehouse door. Mama calls from the other side, "Livy Two, it's late. What are you still doing up?"

"It's summertime. I'm talking to Daddy. He wants applesauce cake right now!"

I can hear Mama still waiting outside the door. Should she haul me outside or let me have my own way? After a moment, she comes around to the window and says, "I'll get his cake, but then it's bedtime. You got to be on the ball tomorrow with Miss Attickson. We've got to stick to a daily routine here, even in summer, or we're sunk, hear me? And I'm taking Grandma's car and going to try to sell my sweaters in Asheville. I'll drop you off at the bookmobile."

I hear her footsteps moving off toward the house. Daddy watches me, only he looks at me sideways, like he's trying to see me better, so I say, "You want a piece of an apple?" I pick one up from the bowl and cut him off a bite with my pocketknife.

"Turn down the radio." He points to the radio while he chews on the apple.

Here we go again. "It's not playing, Daddy."

"I hear the radio. Loud as Christmas!"

I don't know what to tell him, so I ask, "What all do you remember, Daddy?"

"About what?"

The doorknob jiggles, and I call out, "I told you, Mama, I'm staying with Daddy," but it's Louise who answers.

"It's me. Mama said to bring Daddy his cake."

I open it and Louise slips inside the smokehouse.

"Nobody is gonna turn that thing down?" Daddy points to the offending radio that is silent.

Louise sits by Daddy with his cake and asks, "What song is it?"

Daddy listens for a minute. "'Hen Scratchin' Stomp.' That's the tune." Then he eats the cake and the rest of the apple too. He's hungry, but he has a hard time with eating, so Louise helps him. He looks old when he chews. Even older than Grandma Horace. Eating a piece of cake seems like the easiest thing in the world, but he keeps dropping the same bite off his fork, and we have to remind him to swallow sometimes. We don't ever tell people that we still miss him, because then we'll sound crazy, or worse, ungrateful, since he didn't die, but lived and is home with us.

Louise is so easy and patient with Daddy. She treats him like he's the same old person, and has ever since he come home. She pulls out the pad of sketches and shows him the four-leaf clovers pressed between the pages. "See these, Daddy? Remember how you taught us to look for four-leaf clovers all the time when we was little? And fairy hunts too? And you told us Cherokee stories too, remember?"

He says, "'Tennessee Waltz' is blaring on that there radio."

"Daddy," I tell him, "I should buy you a real record player and radio combined. It would take a pile of green stamps, but they got brand-new Philcos on sale at the redemption store. Maybe Mathew the Mennonite could run a line of electricity to the smokehouse."

I hear a noise at the window, and Caroline and Cyrus stretch up their arms to be lifted inside the smokehouse. What I can do? I pull them through the window. Once inside, Cyrus climbs up on the bed to be by Daddy, but Caroline cuddles with Louise.

"Hey, Daddy," Cyrus tells him, "I brought you a present. It's my salamander, Egyptian. He'll keep you company in case you get lonesome. I hope to find a box turtle soon and a frog, and I want to make a cicada necklace for Mama."

Another knock on the door comes. This time, it's Jitters and Becksie with Gentle dragging them both inside with her. Uncle Hazard slips in behind them and jumps up on the bed with Daddy and licks his face. Becksie carries another piece of applesauce cake over to Daddy. She sits with the plate, Jitters next to her. Gentle finds her way to me and crawls into my lap. Daddy's face is one of amazement and confusion.

Cyrus says, "Livy Two, me and Caroline and Gentle put pillows in our beds to fool Mama and Grandma Horace, so we could come out here too. We watched you sneak inside from the window." He looks real pleased with his crafty ways.

The fragrance of cedar and pine warms the room, but we're all still shy around Daddy, so it's an awkward quiet, too, for a room full of kids. The silence in the smokehouse gets louder with Daddy not talking. Who knew that a quieter Daddy would be the loudest sound in the world? Even Becksie notices and says, "Livy Two, I brought out *Gulliver's Travels*. Read some. He was all tied up last time you left off."

Before I can even reach for *Gulliver's Travels*, Grandma Horace looms into the doorway in her robe. "Mercy me, you wild urchins are to leave that poor man in peace to sleep at night. Your mothers has gone to bed herself. Get on to bed now!"

"Please, Grandma Horace? Please! We're being quiet!" The twins cry in unison.

"No discussion." She claps her hands. "I need a full night's rest with my daughter taking off for Asheville tomorrow with sweaters to sell and me left here with the pack. I am earning my angel wings many times over, all I do for you kids! Now, get to bed!"

Everybody drags off back toward the house grumbling, except for me and Gentle. I linger at the door for a moment with her holding my hand. I scoop her up in my arms, and I watch Grandma Horace pick up the spoonful of the applesauce cake and finish feeding Daddy. "Good night, use your napkin, Tom! And swallow, for heaven's sakes!"

We walk to the house in the darkness, and Gentle whispers, "I'm thirsty."

"I'll get you a drink from the springhouse."

Samson, the peacock, lurks by the springhouse, which gives me a start even though he loves to visit us, since he's just the next holler over. He opens up his tail, a magnificent fan of feathers, emerald and indigo. He stands there, waiting to be admired under the summer moon. When he wails his peacock cry, Gentle buries her head against my shoulders, covering her ears.

"Don't be scared. That's just old Samson, letting the world know he's in charge."

"Let me see him," she says, and so I guide her fingers to touch his feathers. He allows a moment of respect and then struts off down the path, feathers plumed like royalty. I give Gentle a dipper of water from an old gourd hollowed out to make a sipping cup. We drink the springwater under the stars and listen to the kids in the house climbing into bed, their voices drifting out of the window.

"Give me my quilt!"

"Say your prayers!"

"I said them!"

"Oh, you lie."

"I said them fast!"

"If you blow up quicksand, is it still quicksand?"

"Quit asking that same question, Caroline Weems! Over and over, I swear!"

As the voices settle, I lean against the springhouse with Gentle in my arms, wishing that I could somehow live in my stories. Wouldn't it be sweet to see a field of fairies swirling over my head, curing Daddy's brain, fixing Gentle's eyes, paying off Madame Cherry Hat, buying us a fine, shiny Philco phonograph player, whispering to Emmett to come home?

Me and Gentle slip inside the house and crawl into bed together. Gentle's heart beats next to mine, and I begin to feel so drowsy, too, like I could sleep for a hundred years. Maybe I can tell some stories to Daddy, think up some funny stories about Uncle Hazard, maybe, since he's the one who brought us our dog way before the accident happened. The way Uncle Hazard begs and looks at us with those pleading eyes, I can imagine him as some kind of wishing hound dog, making wishes to the fairies.

Louise whispers to me in the darkness, Gentle between us, already fast asleep. "Will you bring me a book tomorrow from the bookmobile? Another van Gogh. Or even one about his friend Gauguin. They painted together."

"All right, I will, I will. Now let me sleep."

"Are you listening? You won't forget, will you?" Louise sounds worried.

"I'm awake," I say, but I'm so tired I want to fall into a deep sleep and dream of azalea bushes laced like summer snow around the mountains. I want to dream of the places Miss Attickson will take me come morning. I wonder what Mr. George Flowers will say when he gets my letter. Maybe he'll even want to call me up on the telephone.

CHAPTER TWELVE

Bookmobile Lady

EARLY THE NEXT morning, I scrub up with Ivory soap so I'll be clean for my first day on the job. Mama drops me off at the bookmobile, waving good-bye with a "Cut loose and free for the next few hours" look in her eye. I step up into the bookmobile, parked next to the Maggie School, which is empty because of summer vacation. I climb inside, where I find Miss Attickson placing a bouquet of sunflowers on her desk, which is right behind the driver's seat. When we first moved to Maggie Valley, I used to call it the lending library truck, but everybody around here calls it the bookmobile, so it's rubbed off on me. She glances up and says, "Well, look who it is. My favorite Weems child and every-other-day public servant of Haywood County."

"Hey, Miss Attickson." I feel a little shy all of a sudden because I've been waiting near about forever to see her, and my words get stuck in my throat.

"I'd hire you full-time if I could, but you are twelve years old, and I'm bending the rules as it is!"

"How was your trip home to Memphis? Got your postcard of Beale Street."

"Oh, Olivia!" she starts to say, but then a man stops by to see if we have the latest issue of *Popular Mechanics*. While she's busy with him, I look at my package to Mr. George Flowers. I borrowed a bunch of Grandma Horace's five-cent stamps without her knowing, but I'll pay her back the dollar with my first paycheck. I had to put extra stamps on the box, because it's heavier than a regular envelope with the tape inside. We don't have a reel-to-reel machine to listen to it anyhow, but I know Mr. George Flowers does, so I'm sending it to where maybe it will do some good in the world.

Miss Attickson sends the man off with *Popular Mechanics* and adjusts her red glasses. "I have missed you, Olivia. As for Memphis? It was fine, although Mother about wore me out with several ladies' teas."

"What happens at those things?"

"Not enough, I tell you. They're dull, dull, dull. Finger sandwiches and lemonade and a lot of who's-marrying-who and who's-having-a-baby. Terribly exciting! But do you know what my mother said to me as I was getting ready to leave? She said, 'Do you have to go off to that place again? Can those mountain children even learn?'"

I am insulted at this remark, but Miss Attickson looks just as outraged as me.

"Well, what could I say? It took all the milk of kindness that I could muster, but I said, 'Mother, children are children the world over.' Then I got in my car and was only too happy to head back east to my mountain children."

"Who absolutely can learn!" I give her a hug, it's so good to see her again. Everything smells wonderful—the smell of books and magazines and ink on the printed page. On the board above the checkout desk, Miss Attickson has got some short stories and poems tacked up that kids have sent her from different mountain towns. Miss Attickson says children's stories and poems are her favorite, and she's always having one contest or another to get kids to be storytellers. The latest story on the board is about an Egyptian princess named Nissa from a girl in Canton. Maybe when Cyrus gets older, he'll write Egyptian stories too.

Outside another man raps on the bookmobile door, and it's one of the tobacco farmers from down the road with a wheelbarrow full of books. He calls up, "Howdy to you, Miss Attickson. I come to return my wife's romances and get the new ones. I need to get on back to the fields as I left a no-account brother-in-law in charge, and Lord knows what surprises I'll find when I get back." His broad belly rests on the handle of his wheel-barrow.

She gives me the stack of books to give to him, and I take them outside to him. He nods to me and says, "Thank you kindly, little lady." I hand him the books, picking up the twenty or so in the wheelbarrow.

"Your wife sure must like romance stories," I tell him.

"You don't know the half of it. Bye now." He pushes the wheelbarrow of books down the road, whistling "Brighter Mansion over There."

Once back inside, Miss Attickson hands me a stack of books that need shelving and says, "To tell you the truth, I wasn't sure if you'd be able to work this sum-mer, Olivia, what with your daddy being home again. How's he doing? I've heard all kinds of rumors, but I'd rather hear it from you."

"He's . . . well, he's just fine." But my voice trembles with the lie.

Maybe Miss Attickson answers a little too quickly, "Well, good, then," but she's smart enough not to push it. That's what I love about her. She's not one of those nosy grown-ups who press for details that don't concern them. She wouldn't dream of asking, "Well, what do you mean, he's 'fine,' sugar? Please do explain yourself, and how is your poor poor mother bearing up with all those children?" I hate those nosy grown-ups, who think they're allowed to ask any old question, so they can go off and spread stories everywhere and get them all wrong anyhow.

Besides, how do you explain to someone that your daddy has a radio playing in his head due to auditory hallucinations and that he's prone to mountain wandering? Nope, I'd rather just put my focus on my job here at the bookmobile and leave all the mess back at home. Miss Attickson turns on a record of Mozart, and I like hearing the scratchy recording of his music fill up the bookmobile. I can go with him on his symphonies to faroff places.

I glance at the newspaper headlines of the day. "Valentina Tereshkova, THE FIRST WOMAN IN SPACE." It's her, the one Emmett wrote me about, and it shows a picture of her in her spacesuit heading to the space capsule. The article says she went around the world forty-eight times and lived to tell it. Lucky thing. Law, what did the world look like all those thousands of miles away?

Miss Attickson says, "Today, we'll be heading to Balsam after we're done in Maggie. Tomorrow Saunook. You ready to cover a lot of miles this summer?

Your salary is twenty-five dollars a month, but I hope to be able to give you a little more by summer's end. Can you work three or four days a week, rain or shine?"

"Sounds fine with me. You're not scared to drive in a storm, Miss Attickson?"

"Lord no, folks need their books more than ever when it rains and they're stuck inside all day long. Now keep shelving."

"Yes, ma'am." I get to organizing the books according to subject: fiction, nonfiction, inspirational, children's, and auto mechanics—ABC, ABC, ABC. Then I do my salary in my head. . . . Seventy-five dollars for three months, maybe even a little raise. That's nothing to sneeze at.

Pretty soon, the door to the lending library opens again and again, and kids pour in the door, filled with questions.

"Do you got any Hardy Boys or Nancy Drew?"

"How about *Red Badge of Courage*? Teacher says I got to read it."

"What about Mr. Shakespeare? Where are his collected works?"

The questions never stop. Miss Attickson goes back to making a list of books she needs to order. From time to time, she tells the noisy kids to keep it down, but mostly she's happy to see kids wanting their books, and even some of the kids' mamas ask for magazines like *Ladies' Home Journal* and *McCall's* or the *Burpee's Seed Catalog.* Folks pull wagons and carry pokes to haul the books home. Some mamas want their condensed *Reader's Digest* books, and one lady asks if any F. Scott Fitzgerald books are available, because she wants to read *The Great Gatsby.* Miss Attickson has near about everything, including F. Scott Fitzgerald.

When the crowd clears off around lunchtime, Miss Attickson says, "Shall we head over to Balsam? But we have one stop to make on the way." She starts up the truck, and I sit down next to her in the passenger seat. I look behind me at all the books. As she pulls out onto Highway 19, it's a miracle and a wonder to be driving a roomful of books through the mountains. I'm glad it ain't winter or else we'd likely get stuck in Balsam, as it's the high point in the mountains. The biggest worry when there's snow around here is "Can you get over Balsam?"

I suddenly recollect my package to George Flowers. "Miss Attickson, I got this here package with one of Daddy's new songs, 'Mountain Mint.' The package is a tape reel of me singing last summer at the Mountain Dance and Folk Music Festival. I was wondering if we could mail it at a mailbox today."

"Olivia! Your daddy must be feeling better if he's already writing new songs."

I don't say that he wrote "Mountain Mint" before the car wreck. Instead, I dig my grave deeper and say, "Miss Attickson—it's a miracle. You won't believe it, but he's absolutely fine. It's like nothing ever happened. He's back to his old self. In fact, I think he drove himself to three banjo auditions yesterday and sold a heap of baby-food jars and a few sets of encyclopedias."

"Why, that's such wonderful news," Miss Attickson says, but I get gnawing feeling in my gut.

"Isn't it the best?" I hope my voice doesn't sound as strangled as it feels. "But I really do need to mail this today, and if it's all right with you, I'd like to use the bookmobile as a return address. Mama and Grandma Horace don't think too much of the Nashville music men since they told Daddy 'no' so much. But they don't get how a songwriter has to keep trying! It might take a hundred 'no's before you get a 'yes,' right?"

Then I hear a cough from the far end of the book-mobile deep behind the stacks. Did a kid forget to get off? Why do I know that familiar cough?

Miss Attickson hears it too and asks, "Is there a stray child lurking back there? Show yourself. We won't bite."

After a moment, Louise steps out from behind the stacks with a sheepish look on her face, which means she's heard every lying, skunky word to cross my lips.

"When did you sneak onboard, Miss Louisiana Weems?" Miss Attickson shifts into low gear as we near a stop sign, not at all rattled by our new passenger.

Louise knows Miss Attickson and loves her too, because last year, Miss Attickson gave her a set of paints, which Louise had to use to pour all over these hornets that swarmed Uncle Hazard, but when Miss Attickson heard about it, she sent her up some new ones. So Louise trusts Miss Attickson and is not too scared to talk to her.

She stammers, "I—I—I come in with a pile of kids. Y'all just didn't see. I'm like Invisible Kid."

"Very clever," Miss Attickson congratulates Louise.

"Then I got busy reading this here tourist guide about Ghost Town. Carved out seventy feet of mountain to make it and—" Her eyes glued to the floor, she stammers, "But, never mind . . . but . . . I needed another van Gogh book and a Gauguin. I was afraid Livy Two might forget and I—oh. Anyhow, I—"

"Finish your sentences, would you? And I didn't forget!" But I had forgotten all about it until this very second.

"Since you're here now, would you like to come along with us today?" Miss Attickson invites her without asking me a word about it, so I blurt out, "I guess she already has! Does Grandma Horace know you're here since Mama's gone to Asheville?"

"She, um . . . Grandma Horace said you forgot your lunch. She made an applesauce cake for Miss Attickson. Take it."

"Well, that's lovely." Miss Attickson nods, eyes on the road. "We'll have a picnic in Balsam. Isn't that the prettiest name for a town? Sometimes, I wonder about the folks who thought up all these pretty mountain names: Balsam, Sapphire, Snowbird Mountain. It's poetry, pure poetry."

"What's poetry about Clyde or Enka?" I ask in a low voice, but Miss Attickson ignores my ugly remark.

Louise says, "Livy Two, you want me to get off and . . . or . . . ? 'Cause I—"

I interrupt, "It's a free country." But I don't meet her eye, so she knows I'm not happy. The bookmobile job is mine, and I don't aim to share it, not even with my beloved sister, Louisiana Weems.

"Louise, I was just asking your sister about your daddy and hearing of his miraculous return to songwriting." Miss Attickson takes the turn toward Waynesville.

Louise flashes a look at me before she says, "Yes, ma'am. I heard every word."

About nine miles or so out of Maggie Valley, Miss Attickson pulls up to a stop on a dirt road and asks me to leave a stack of old *National Geographic* magazines at a house yonder. It could hardly be called a real house, more of a shotgun shack, and an ugly one at that—a room on stacks of bricks with a few steps leading up to the front door is more like.

"He's a shy man who lives there," Miss Attickson explains, "so just leave everything on the steps and get on back here. These are old *National Geographic* magazines that I give him to keep, since there's no room on the bookmobile for them."

Louise says, "I'll help too," and since it's a big stack, I let her. Together, we climb down out of the bookmobile to set the magazines on the step. She whispers to me, "That was a pack of whoppers you told about Daddy. I was even beginning to believe it the way you made it sound all roses." I ignore her and call back to Miss Attickson. "Who lives here anyhow?"

But before she can answer, the door opens, and it's Billy O'Connor, who takes one look at me and dives back inside. Then the sunken face of Pokey McPherson appears. "Who wants to know? What do you want?" he snarls at me like a fenced-up yard dog. "I'll get you for trespassing. I'm off bus duty for the entire summer, and when I'm off duty, I don't want to see any stinking bus kids around my property. No troublemakers!"

"What's Billy O'Connor doing in there then?" I ask him.

"None of your business! Nosy Weems kid!" When his hot vinegar breath hits my face I duck, and Louise practically leaps back on the bookmobile in a single shot. He sees the bookmobile and changes his tune. "Howdy, Miss Attickson. Caught these kids snooping around my property. You can be my witness."

"Hello, Mr. McPherson," Miss Attickson replies in a cool voice. "I certainly will be your witness. Olivia and Louise were just dropping off your stack of *National Geographic* as you requested. Olivia works for me, and if you are interested in receiving materials from our Haywood County Library, I will need you to speak with more decorum to my employee, and to her sister, who is along for today."

"Your employee? That smart-mouthed kid?"

"That's right. How is your nephew doing?"

"Billy? Tolerable. His mama's got the fits again. They say she gets it from dipping too much snuff, but I know she was born with it, snuff or no snuff."

"I'm sorry to hear that. When she's feeling better, give her my regards."

"You pay her?" Pokey scratches his head.

"I do, indeed."

"How much?" He looks at me like he can't hardly believe it—like anybody who'd offer me a nickel would have to be crazy. "Never mind. Just give me my *National Geographic*s then."

"Here, take them." I pick up the magazines that Louise has dropped and hand them to him.

"Good-bye." He shuts the door in my face, but I see Billy peeking through a thin curtain in the window.

"You're welcome!" I call before I get back on the bookmobile, where Louise is still shivering from fright. How can she kill copperheads in broad daylight but be afraid of somebody like Pokey McPherson? After we drive a few miles toward Balsam, I spy a postbox. "Could you pull over, please, Miss Attickson?"

Miss Attickson parks the bookmobile on the side of the road, and I hop out to mail the package to Mr. George Flowers. Louise never says a word about it, so I know she won't give away my secret to Mama or Grandma Horace. When I get back inside, I ask Miss Attickson, "What's Pokey McPherson want with a bunch of *National Geographic* magazines? I didn't even know that man could read."

Miss Attickson signals to turn and says, "I expect Mr. McPherson can read enough to get by. He has to read the road signs, otherwise they never would have given him the job."

"Well, me and Louise run to school now to keep off that mean yellow school bus. We've gotten good at running together instead of being on that bus. Louise is fastest."

"Maybe you girls will join the track team at Waynesville High School when you're old enough, but I wouldn't be too hard on Mr. McPherson or his nephew."

"I would," I mutter, but Louise says, "Hush! Why not?"

"They're lonesome folks. From what I've seen, Mr. McPherson lets Billy tinker with car engines behind the house. Y'all ever hear of Henry David Thoreau? He lived way out in nature to get away from the world . . . and he wrote about how most men lead lives of quiet desperation. I believe that's your bus driver too."

Lives of quiet desperation? Our snarling, speedy bus driver who hauls busloads of kids through the mountains day after day? It don't fit the picture I have of him at all. Maybe his meanness is tied up in traveling miles and miles every day but always ending up in the same place?

As Miss Attickson takes the road to Balsam, Louise asks her, "Are you leading a life of quiet desperation?"

"Certainly not." Miss Attickson tucks a loose strand of hair behind her ear. "I have my books."

Later that afternoon, when we get back to Maggie Valley, I say to Miss Attickson, "I need a book. A book on brains. I lied earlier. My daddy is not himself yet, and

I'd like to get a book on brains to study up on how to help him."

Miss Attickson says, "Why couldn't you tell me that in the first place, Olivia?"

I hang my head, scarlet with shame, but Louise says, "Our daddy—he will be well . . . soon enough. But he's not. Not yet. Livy Two meant he will be. Better. Soon."

Miss Attickson ponders this explanation for a moment before she says, "Well, I guess I'd better special order some books on Vincent van Gogh and Paul Gauguin and one on the human brain. I did remember Gentle's Braille books. I picked her out some good ones: *A Time of Wonder, One Morning in Maine*, and *A Child's Garden of Verses*. Oh, and here are Emmett's *Adventure Comics*. I do not know what he sees in them, but at least he's reading something! And take these Cicely Mary Barker books to Caroline, and here's *King Tut* for Cyrus. And Nancy Drew for Jitters and Becksie. And what the heck, let's get Emmett to try a Hardy Boys too."

"Thank you, Miss Attickson!" And with that, we grab the sack of books, and me and Louise race up the road to our holler, our feet barely touching the ground we run so fast. A song of the bookmobile floats in my head as our feet pound the earth with books in our arms.

Bookmobile Lady

Bookmobile lady, driving stories through the mountains,
Bookmobile lady, tales and tales rain down in fountains,
Folks with wheelbarrows, wagons, totes, and sacks
All for to haul the books home on their backs . . .
Bookmobile lady, holding secrets of the hollers . . .
Bookmobile lady . . .
Bookmobile lady, she's got mountains to roam
Then drive your lending library truck home. . . .

CHAPTER THIRTEEN

Lighthouse Fairy Tale

THE WEEKS PASS with me working every other day with Miss Attickson, but still no word from Mr. George Flowers. I bring home my first twenty-five dollars for Mama, who looks pleased and puts it in the CASH & PAY-CHECKS envelope inside the Everything Box. Mama's got money to add to it, too, since she's sold some of her "Jessie's Mountain Sweaters" over in Asheville to a consignment shop. When the check arrives from Asheville, she drops it right in the Everything Box, along with Becksie's tips and paychecks, Grandma Horace's Social Security check, and Emmett's hit-or-miss contributions. Every so often Grandma Horace drives the thirty miles to make a deposit into the Enka bank where she's banked all her life—there's no sense in changing now, as she calls herself a temporary guest in Haywood County.

But money is still tight, and Mama wants to get

Daddy some kind of therapy to help him with the radio in his head and his memory, and that's more money. Plus it's almost time for Gentle's eyes to be examined again, and none of us have been to the dentist except for once in our lives. Mama makes us floss our teeth with string or matchbooks or willow twigs—whatever we can find—and we brush every day with baking soda, but I know she's wanting us to get to a dentist for cleaning, and that won't come cheap. As for regular doctor visits? Mama says she doesn't need a doctor to tell her that her children are healthy. It's like all the things that Daddy used to say are now coming out of her mouth, while he practices remembering.

She has that haunted look in her eye about money, so I'm relieved that the summer garden's in full bloom with summer squash, tomatoes, green peppers, carrots, and sweet peas. Grandma Horace has canned some tomatoes and summer squash to keep in the root cellar, which she claims is the most useful room in this whole holler. She calls it "the underground grocery store for Weems children." Every time the electricity gets cut off when we're late with the bill or a check bounces, at least we got the root cellar, the springhouse, and the woodstove. But she's not giving up on Enka-Stinka either, and she actually called up the principal of the school over there to have him send some information about the elementary school. When it arrives, I throw it in the trash.

Uncle Hazard barks at the crows and chases off the raccoons and other critters who'd like to feast on our winter's food. Louise works in the garden every day, and sometimes, Ruth comes over to help, too, if her daddy says yes. They seem like they're becoming friends, and sometimes I feel flashes of jealousy when I see them laughing at something together. I figured Ruth to be my friend first, what with Louise being so shy. I figured wrong. I still ain't found the right time to show Louise the "Greetings from Louisiana" postcard, but I do drop little reminder notes on her pillow that say "Waynesville Portraits by up-and-coming artist Louisiana Weems!"

Daddy seems no better or worse, and I begin to wonder if this is the daddy we're stuck with. When I ask Mama what she thinks, she says, "Livy Two, I lost my daddy when I was real young to the cancer. Grandma Horace had to raise me up as best she could all alone, and that's why she's the way she is. You got to be patient with both her and your daddy. Understand? Be grateful that your daddy is here. He's different now, darling, but he's here." Then she hugs me and says, "Now, go to sleep and dream sweet dreams."

And night after night, I dream of Daddy. . . . One

night in my dream, he comes to me just like nothing ever happened and says, "How are you, my sweet Magnolia Blossom, baby?" And I say, "Just fine, Daddy. Me and Emmett are going fishing—you want to come?" Daddy says, "Fishing? Why, I'd love to catch me a big bass. What are we waiting on?" And then me, Daddy, and Emmett are fishing in a boat over on Lake Junaluska with the sun beating down on our backs. The fish are biting, and we keep catching them—bass, trout, catfish. On a transistor radio nearby on another boat, the silky voice of Patsy Cline sings "Crazy." Daddy is laughing and catching fish after fish, yelling, "Look out! Hand me that can of night crawlers. Wait, here comes another fish." I say, "How are we going to eat all this fish?" Emmett says, "We'll have a giant fish fry up on Waterrock Knob and invite the fairies," and Daddy laughs, and so I ask him, "Is your head all right?" And he says, "You kidding me? Darling, I'm fine. I'm fishing with my kids. What could be better? How'd I get so lucky?" Me and Emmett laugh. I cling to the threads of the dream, trying to memorize it, because it's been so long since I've been safe with Daddy and my brother, laughing and telling stories, serenaded by Patsy Cline.

Something jerks me awake, and I find Gentle, Cyrus, and Caroline sitting plum on top of me in the bunk bed. The straw ticking from the old mattress sticks me in the back, too, so I'm getting jabbed from all sides. They've even got Uncle Hazard up in the bed. He licks my face, tail wagging *good morning!* His dog breath reeks of old cow-pies. Louise is squished against the wall, in a deep sleep in spite of the intruders.

"What are y'all doing?" I hiss at them. "Go back to bed before Grandma Horace knocks the tar out of you! I got to work soon."

"No, it's Saturday. You never play with us no more," Caroline accuses. "Ever!"

"I do too, but it's the middle of the night!" I yawn. "Good night!"

"No, it ain't either. The sun's coming up!" Cyrus says. "See there?"

And sure enough, the sky outside the window is turning a crest of cotton-candy pink above the mountains. "It's still the crack of dawn."

Gentle bounces on the bed. "Wake up! Caroline had a bad dream about Daddy. She woke me up, and I woke up Cyrus. Now it's your turn. Get up! Come on."

"Come cuddle with me, all of you. . . . You're getting very, very, very sleepy." I try to coax them under the covers to rest a little more, but nothing doing.

Cyrus spreads his arms out wide. "Livy Two, I dreamed about the ocean! What's the strongest fish in it? A killer whale or a great white shark? Who'd win the fight?"

"Maybe it would be a tie." Gentle brushes her hair with a little comb.

Caroline shudders. "I dreamed a monster swallowed me whole. No chewing, just swallowing. I told him to eat me to make the dream be over."

"Oh, honey, it was a dream. Y'all go back to bed!" I burrow under the covers.

"No!" Gentle beats her little fists softly on my back. "You promised to play yesterday!" I try to cover my head with my pillow, but the twins pull it back off. "A promise is a promise!" Gentle whispers in my ear.

Caroline cries, "Livy Two don't care about promises anymore!"

"Maybe she does," Cyrus defends me. "Maybe she means to care."

It's no use, and I can't yell at them or risk waking up the whole house, and I know they've missed me 'cause I used to play with them, but it's like I quit somehow. All three have pairs of eyes like blue violets and hair the color of goldenrod, except the twins have more red in their hair like Louise, while Gentle's is more yellow with streaks of honey like Mama's. Her violet eyes are different too—they concentrate. If eyes could listen, that is what Gentle's eyes do.

Gentle says, "I can hear fairy wings in the garden and in the barn."

"No, them are dragonflies or butterflies or maybe bats," Cyrus corrects her.

"Not bats, no! Fairies, Cyrus!" Gentle's lower lip trembles, and Caroline yells, "Real fairies! We'll find some on our fairy hunt up on Waterrock Knob and prove it. How high is it again?"

"Over six thousand feet . . . and there's all kinds of fairies up there—granddaddy fairies, old aunt fairies, pretty baby fairies, tooth fairies, flower fairies, everything!"

Caroline points at him. "They got soft wings, and at night the pixies come and tie tangles and knots in our hair. They like tricks."

"I heard that fairies is mostly for girls?" Cyrus says it like a question.

"Why, don't you know that Daddy's seen more fairies than anybody? Who do you think started the fairy hunts? It wasn't Mama or Grandma Horace, that's for sure."

"You think the fairies helped me find the cicada shells so I could make that necklace for Mama?" Cyrus asks after a minute.

"Who else do you think?" I ask him. "They even visit Uncle Hazard, I bet."

Cyrus says, "Then let's get off this bed now and go find some!"

"Wait," I whisper. "So y'all think this is a bed? That's what you think? Boy, are you wrong! Why, this here is no bed! We're at the top of a lighthouse, and out there is the Maggie Valley Harbor full of killer whales and great white sharks!" I point out the window. "Can you hear the crashing waves? Taste the smell of salty sea air. Try!"

"I'm listening for the ships!" Gentle whispers. "The seagulls are cawing."

Caroline and Cyrus cry, "And we're standing guard for pirates!"

Becksie rolls over on her bunk. "No, no more pancakes! Too many pancakes!"

"That's right," Jitters says in her sleep. "No pancakes, please."

The little ones giggle, and I say, "I reckon you'uns want to hear how Uncle Hazard, our famous dog, made a lighthouse wish so he could keep folks safe from pirates and killer sharks? But if I tell it, you reckon you can howl like a long-eared hot dog with a snuffly nose? Only you got to howl soft since folks are sleeping and might get scared."

Caroline, Gentle, and Cyrus howl, as soft as they can, *Barrooo! Barrooo!*

Uncle Hazard joins them too: *Barrooo! Barrooo!*

And so at the crack of dawn, to make up for not playing with the little ones in just about forever, I make up the very first story about how Uncle Hazard became the wishingest hot dog of Maggie Valley. I call it "Lighthouse."

Gather round, young'uns, to hear the tale of Uncle Hazard, the wishingest hot dog in the misty mountains of Maggie Valley, who woke up one morning with an idea buzzing around in his brain. Uncle Hazard stretched, yawned, and shook his floppy ears—*flap, flap, flap, flappity, flap*—outside his pinecone palace and bayed, *Barrooo! Barrooo!* It all started when his best friend, Louisiana Margaret Pansy Jeanne Marie Weems—Louise for short—brought home a picture book of ships sailing across the ocean blue from the bookmobile. It weren't so much the proud sails, steady rudders, and frothy ocean that caught Uncle Hazard's attention, for Uncle Hazard hated water and baths with a passion. But try as he might, he could not quit thinking about that tall beacon of light on the rocky shores in one of the photographs.

Uncle Hazard howled out his questions to

Louise, who understood dog language better than any young'un who roamed the hills and hollers of Maggie Valley. She twisted a lock of curly red hair around a finger and said, "Why, Uncle Hazard, that there's a lighthouse. It lights up at night and during storms to help lost ships find their way home."

Barrooo! Barrooo! Uncle Hazard bawled. His hot-dog heart beat something wild. He imagined how it would feel to be a lighthouse on the rocky shores of the ocean. It seemed a perfect thing to be as long as he wouldn't have to get wet. All that day in the holler, he thought and wished and dreamt of how to become a lighthouse that saved lost sailors and ships at sea from storms, great white sharks, killer whales, and lurking pirate ships. See, Uncle Hazard wanted to be a true live hero on a grand adventure instead of some old wiener dog living in a mountain holler.

That night, all the Weems children went to bed in their bunk beds, and several of the Weems babies went to sleep in their dresser drawers since there weren't near enough cribs for all the babies. Soon everyone was sleeping, except for Louise, who brought a piece of cornbread and a bowl of buttermilk out to Uncle Hazard for a midnight snack. As he and Louise curled up together, Uncle Hazard made a wish under the milky moon and stars. All was silent in the holler except for the chirp of crickets who weren't the least bit sleepy and a crowd of cicadas giving a concert down by the creek. But as night deepened, Uncle Hazard's wishes traveled up into the secret crevices of the mountains around Maggie Valley. Soon the mountain fairies from up near Waterrock Knob came buzzing out the bluffs, swirling on breezes that carried the notions of a wishing hot dog.

When Louise opened her eyes, thousands of gossamer wings like a whirlpool of fireflies greeted her in the midnight-blue blackness, but these mountain fairies appeared befuddled, which means mighty head-scratching confused. In fact, one fairy did scratch her head, another blew her nose, and a third batted his wings and yodeled, "Lighthouse?"

The mountain fairies did the only thing they could think of—they called upon their ocean fairy cousins at Myrtle Beach, who heard their cry and whirled across the state of North Carolina in a pool of ivory light, bringing the Atlantic Ocean on their backs.

As the fairies arrived with the ocean, Uncle Hazard found his long hot-dog body stretching taller and taller toward the starry night. When he was more than a hundred and fifty feet tall, he realized his head was the top of the lighthouse, and his body was the lighthouse itself, with sand dunes and grasses snuggled all around him. Once in a while, a wave slapped his black toe-nail ocean rocks and his lighthouse belly, which tickled Uncle Hazard, but he decided to be brave even with the water inching so close.

Louise called to her brothers and sisters, and the whole passel of Weems young'uns awoke from their dreams and did leaping somersaults off the sand dunes. As the Weems children clambered up near two hundred steps, they peeked out of Uncle Hazard's head, now the lighthouse window, and feasted their eyes on the sparkling sapphire ocean for the very first time in their lives.

Ah, this is the life! Uncle Hazard thought as he opened his mouth to sound a lonesome foghorn for any ships lost at sea. And then right through his hot-dog nose, a beam of light shone out across the midnight waters to guide the ships home and away from a white shark, circling round and round. The Weems children grabbed their ears when Uncle Hazard's foghorn mouth sounded, *Barrooo! Barrooo!* That old horn was so loud it seemed to rattle their bones and wallop their eardrums.

But as you can imagine, when the good folks of Maggie Valley awoke, they were mighty stirred up to discover the ocean arrived at their own back door. The pancake maker of Maggie Valley sailed by on a raft filled with soggy mountain blackberry pancakes, shouting, "Hey, Uncle Hazard, you old hot dog! What in creation is going on here?"

The bookmobile of Maggie Valley turned into a bookmobile ship, but it pitched and rocked so much that all the children got seasick reading their books. And all the cloggers, whittlers, and dollmakers of Maggie Valley had one heck of a time clogging, whittling, and dollmaking with so much ocean water, brine, and curious fish everywhere.

After Uncle Hazard saved a few ships from a watery doom, and scared off some pirates with his blasting foghorn, he had his fill of being a heroic hot-dog lighthouse, so the fairies went to work. The mountain fairies and ocean fairies flew the Weems children back safely to their beds (and dresser drawers) and tucked them into a deep sleep. Then the mountain fairies shrank Uncle Hazard back down to size, and the ocean fairies hauled the Atlantic Ocean back across the mountains with them and put it back where it belonged. Naturally, it took some weeks for the good folks of Maggie Valley to squeeze the salt water out of their clothes and scrape the seaweed from their ears, but soon life returned to normal.

Even Uncle Hazard stretched and yawned and shook his floppy ears—*flap, flap, flap, flappity, flap*—outside his pinecone palace each morning when he woke up. But it wasn't too long before he was thinking up a brand-new idea in his heroic hot-dog brain . . . because that's just what those wishing hot dogs do when they greet each day with a *Barrooo!*, seeking out new ways to be heroes and have adventures!

As I finish the story, Caroline cries, "Tell it again!" while Cyrus and Gentle keep howling, *Barrooo! Barrooo!*

Louise, awake now, was propped up on her elbow listening to every word. Then she says, "Oceans, fairies, sharks, killer whales, pirates, and lighthouses? Livy Two, I might could paint the world of that crazy story sometime. Could you remember it?"

"Sure I can . . . and I can make up plenty more Uncle Hazard stories for you."

With the little ones busy howling to the ceiling, Louise whispers into my ear, "I know what let's do. We could make a book of your lighthouse fairy tale for the twins' birthday and for Gentle too. They're just a month apart. We could make a real pretty one, since you know there won't be money for presents. We'll give them an 'Uncle Hazard Fairy Tale.' I'll paint it, you supply the words."

I nod real quick, but the twins have quit howling and are now looking at us with great suspicion. A smile plays on Gentle's lips like she's got a secret too. Caroline points an accusing finger. "You're telling secrets about us."

Gentle says, "I know the secret. Do you want a hint?"

I snap, "Gentle Weems, if you do tell or even give a hint, I'll be so mad."

Gentle giggles. "You should know by now that I hear everything. I have superpower hearing like Super Boy in Emmett's stories, but I won't tell."

Grandma Horace calls, "Breakfast! Shake a leg! And there's a surprise out here waiting for you!"

We'd have to be stone deaf not to hear that direct order, and nobody needs to be called twice for a meal in this house even if it's just plain oatmeal. Becksie and Jitters struggle awake under the warm covers, and I can hear the babies fussing for their breakfast. What's the surprise, I wonder as I yank on my overalls and head to the kitchen. Law, I can't wait to write the fairy tale with Louise painting the pictures. Wait till I tell Miss Attickson! I'd like to tell Daddy too, but frankly, I don't think he would care so much. He might say, "What? Who? Uncle Hazard? Who's that?" It's hard to have to explain everything over and over again to your own father. Not only is he missing his words—sometimes, I think he even forgot he has ten kids.

CHAPTER FOURTEEN

Daddy's Missing Piece

LOUD, ACCUSING VOICES lash through the air from the kitchen, which make me and Louise stop short and hold the little ones at bay. From the doorway, our brother Emmett sits big as life at the kitchen table, while Mama's giving him what-for in a voice shot clean with icicles. "All I got to say is that you took your sweet time coming home to see your daddy. Then I wake up this morning to see you sprawled out sound asleep on the sofa in the front room like some creature from the black lagoon."

"I been working. I didn't want to wake nobody up. Good to see you too, Mama."

"Don't you get smart with me!"

"Well, geez, it takes three hours to walk home at night in the dark and first thing you do is bite my dang head off!"

The kids squirm in my arms to get to Emmett, but I

hold on tight because Mama's slamming things around in there, which means "Enter at Your Own Risk!"

"Would you care to explain your absence, then? Why my calls to Ghost Town went unreturned?" Mama slaps breakfast bowls on the table with baby Tom-Bill on her hip. Appelonia sits in her chair beaming at Emmett and playing peekaboo with him.

"Mama, please . . . they never give days off, not if you want the hundred-dollar bonus come the end of summer."

"Bonus? That's a good one." She keeps right on talking, almost to herself. "You could have walked home!"

"Well, I'm a working man, Mama, with duties and responsibilities. Besides, I went up to Amish country to get a stagecoach for Ghost Town. Way up in Ohio. I had to help load it." Emmett covers his eyes, making Appelonia explode in giggles.

The little ones try to push by me, but I whisper to them, "Wait! They're having a big important talk, so just hush up and wait."

"Pin a ribbon on you with your fine duties and responsibilities!" Mama snaps. "Such important work in Amish country! Far more important than the likes of us."

Emmett's ears redden; his jaw gets set tight. "Look, I can leave. I don't have to stay. I got my own life now, and I can go right back to it."

"Then go. Who needs you here? You were going

to send money. You had all kinds of big plans to send money. Instead, it's a pitiful ten here, ten there. I depended on you, Emmett, and you let me down. You let us all down hard."

"I'm sorry, Mama. I can explain if you—"

"Sorry is not enough this time. Not near enough." Her voice has got a jagged tear.

"What happened to you, Mama?"

"What happened to me?" She whirls around to face Emmett. "I tell you what happened—life happened, Emmett!" She pats baby Tom-Bill, who's got the hiccups, on the back before she sets him down in the wicker basket on the floor and grips the kitchen sink like she can't hardly stand it. "Why didn't you come home before now? Why? Say it."

Emmett gets quiet, and I'm mad at Mama for giving him such a hard time.

"I hate Daddy sick. Satisfied? I hate it. But I'm here today to take the kids to Ghost Town. I got free passes, and I wanted to do something to make up for everything. I done told you last year the accident was my fault. I hit the rockslide, and—"

Mama can't hold back the tears. "Lord, then take the children to Ghost Town. I'm so blamed tired. Take the whole family, son, if that's all you come to do."

Grandma Horace comes into the kitchen and says,

"Now, now, what's all this high drama, Jessie, at this hour? Why don't you go rest? You didn't sleep much last night. Emmett, this is pure exhaustion talking in your mama."

Mama says, "It feels like I've been awake a hundred years or more. Maybe we should move back to Enka. That's what Mama wants, Emmett. You know that? I could get a job at Champion Paper or American Enka with benefits. I'm near out of sweaters. I need time to make more—never enough time, but we all thought that Daddy would be . . ." She swallows a sob because she don't believe in crying in front of kids.

Emmett says, "Mama," and he reaches into his pocket and lays fifty dollars on the table. "More is coming, I swear. I had to learn to stand up to Uncle Buddy. I didn't know I could before." He turns to Grandma Horace and says, "I kept quiet 'cause I didn't want to worry you, but besides making birdhouses, your brother is a poker cheat."

Grandma Horace shakes her head and says, "Yes, my brother bears watching. I knew it. I told you so, Jessie."

Mama sits at the table, wore out—like she's done ten years of living in this one last year. She takes the money and puts it in her pocket. "Thank you, son."

"You're welcome. I know I could have done better, and I'm sorry."

"You're fifteen. I guess I remember fifteen a little."
Mama's anger has drained away, replaced by weari-
ness. "But, darling, you've been missed more than
you know." She wipes a tear away, and then I can't
hold the little ones back any longer, and they fly
into the kitchen to hug on Emmett. "Are we rich as
kings?" Gentle cries as Caroline and Cyrus climb all
over Emmett.

"Hey, look who got big? Who wants to go to Ghost
Town?"

"We do, we do!" the little ones shriek. "Emmett's
home, Emmett came back!"

"I want to ride the chairlift," Gentle says, "and go
way, way, way up in the air like Uncle Hazard when he
grew up into a lighthouse."

Emmett cocks his head confused, but right then,
Becksie and Jitters come into the kitchen and stop short,
shocked to see Emmett back among the fold.

Becksie says, "You're back? Guess what? I'm queen
of Maggie School and I got a job at the Pancake House!
How about them apples?"

"Yes, she's queen!" Jitters nods. "For all of eighth
grade coming up. It's so exciting!"

Emmett says, "I heard. I also heard Evie Pepper
wasn't too thrilled about it."

"How do you know that?" Becksie pours herself a

cup of coffee, a new habit ever since she started her job at the Pancake House.

"Evie Pepper's mother works at the Mad Hatter at Ghost Town," Emmett says, "Boy, you'd-a thought the world was ending as we know it. But congratulations."

Becksie and Jitters smile in spite of themselves, and Grandma Horace says, "Eat up now, children, and Emmett, you may as well tell us the news of Uncle Buddy."

Emmett whistles a long whistle like he don't know whether to tell or not.

"What'd he do this time?" Louise feeds Appelonia and baby Tom-Bill, who reaches for Emmett's yellow hair, sticking out in a million directions.

Emmett's eyes get real big when he tells the story, and he uses his hands when he talks, and I can't help but notice how much he looks like a man now and not a boy. "A few weeks back"—Emmett tries to keep from grinning—"Uncle Buddy thought he spied an escaped gorilla running around Ghost Town on the loose from a traveling circus in Waynesville. He turned on the park alarms, flashing lights, and got on the speaker yelling, 'Wild gorilla! Danger! Lock your doors!'"

"A real gorilla?" Gentle wants to know.

"Hang on . . . I'll tell you. . . . So Uncle Buddy was running around like a chicken with his head cut off, and he even called up the sheriff in Maggie Valley to get on the case."

The little kids lean forward to hear the rest of the story, eating bite after bite of oatmeal laced with black-strap molasses. Emmett slaps his knee. "Turned out to be one of the gunslingers dressed in a gorilla costume. Uncle Buddy won't ever live that one down 'cause they run a story about it in the *Smoky Mountain News*."

Everybody bursts out laughing, picturing Uncle Buddy chasing this way and that all because of a fake gorilla, but a stomping quiets us from the front porch and soon Daddy stands in the doorway to the kitchen. He doesn't notice Emmett at first and says, "Where's my breakfast? A man could starve here. A man—" But he stops when he lays eyes on Emmett. You could hear a pin drop in that kitchen as we wait to see what Daddy will do. For the first since he's come home, his face lights up into a big Daddy grin like the old days, and I breathe a huge sigh of relief. He knows him. He knows Emmett. "Look at you!" Daddy hugs on him, which is like to embarrass Emmett to death, since he's not a hugging boy.

Red-faced, Emmett says, "You want to go to Ghost Town? Got free passes!"

Daddy sits down in a chair. "Ghost Town. What's that mean? Ghost Town."

Emmett laughs. "You pulling my leg, Daddy?"

But he's not joking, so Louise says, "Daddy, they built this park on top of Buck Mountain. They started in September of sixty-one and it was opened in the spring of sixty-two. It's been open a full year now. Took twenty thousand pounds of nails to build."

"How do you know that?" Becksie says. "Why would you even know that?"

"I read about it in the bookmobile. They also needed twenty-one thousand feet of steel railways for the incline cars," Louise adds, "and the chairlift can carry seventeen hundred folks up and down the mountain per hour."

Emmett says, "Shoot, you ought to be a tour guide, Louise!"

"I just like to read how folks put things together, and Daddy needs pictures in his head to make him remember things. I finally figured it out, and that's why I keep making more flashcards." She turns to Daddy. "Right? If I give you a picture instead of a fact, you remember better."

Daddy says, "Ghost Town. Where is that place? Far off?"

Emmett looks stunned. "Right here in Maggie Valley. Is your memory that bad?"

"If I knew, I'd tell you." Daddy laughs, and this time it

is a joke. His first. It's like Emmett is the piece he's been missing, because he's truly trying to keep up and talk.

Emmett shakes his head. "So y'all want to go to Ghost Town?"

Becksie says, "I have to work at the Pancake House. Will you leave me a pass?"

"Sure I will," Emmett laughs. "I'll leave it right by the sign in the Ghost Town ticket office that says, NO REFUNDS, NO EXCHANGES, NO RAIN CHECKS."

Mama looks at me and says, "Is Miss Attickson wanting you today?"

"Tomorrow. It's every other day, Mama." I turn to Louise. "You going with us?" But she don't answer except to shrug and eat her breakfast.

"Well, I am going!" Daddy says. "Where is it again?"

"It would be a long day for you, Tom," Grandma Horace says, and gets Daddy breakfast.

"I'm going to that place!" Daddy says. "I am going. What's it called again?"

"Ghost Town! Hooray, us too!" The twins scramble up from the table to get ready.

"Can I taste cotton candy?" Gentle pleads. "Please?"

Grandma Horace says, "I expect we can fit in the station wagon if we sit on laps."

Mama says, "Will y'all kids keep on eye on your

daddy? Because I'm not going. I'll keep the babies. I'm too tired to see straight."

Louise says, "Mama, I'll stay and help you. Besides, Ruth might visit today."

"You can see Ruth any day—please come?" I beg. Not to mention I'll be the one stuck watching Daddy the whole time if she stays home, and she's better at it than me.

"Too many folks for me up there, Livy Two," Louise says, her mind made up, but Emmett looks real disappointed, because Ghost Town is his big present for all of us.

Grandma Horace says, "Well I, for one, am not missing a trip to Ghost Town. I have a thing or two to say to my brother about poker debts and stealing from boys."

Emmett stands up and says, "You sure you won't change your mind, Louisiana Weems? You could pretend the crowd is all aliens belonging to Lightning Lad or Invisible Kid or Saturn Girl or Cosmic Boy. What do you say? There's so much to show you. Say yes, come on!"

But Louise won't be coaxed into Ghost Town, not for nothing!

CHAPTER FIFTEEN

Ghost Town in the Sky

EMMETT HELPS DADDY get dressed in regular clothes, which hang on him, but Emmett tightens the belt, and smoothes out the trousers and shirt. Daddy looks like a real person again, not wearing that brown bathrobe. Only I can't believe how skinny he is.

"Last chance, Louise?" I ask, but right then, Ruth appears from behind a cypress tree near the fence joining the top of our two hollers. Louise races over to her without giving us so much as a backward glance. Hot flames of jealousy lick at my heart as we pile into Grandma Horace's car and head toward the foot of Buck Mountain on Highway 19. When we get to the parking lot, I notice the sky is a lilac color, so I study the clouds to see if the storm is gonna get us or not. Emmett notices and kneels down to the little ones. "Guess what? Did you know that sometimes it can be raining down in Maggie Valley, and not a drop up will hit us on top of Buck Mountain?"

Grandma Horace also examines the sky. I guess she decides it will behave, because soon enough, we're riding up Buck Mountain in the chairlift, the tree tops far below us.

Caroline says, "Look at the sky . . . just like Louise's words for purple. Lavender, violet, orchid."

"And grape, too, don't forget!" Cyrus says.

"Purple is the air before it rains," Gentle says, and with that, little fat drops begin falling on our arms and faces. "Purple's my favorite color."

How can Gentle truly have a favorite color if she's never even seen colors? But maybe Louise has given her enough of an idea through the other senses. *Green is rolling in the grass, yellow is the sun on your back, red is the woodstove baking up biscuits . . .*

"A little rain never hurt nobody!" Emmett yells back to us from the chair ahead, where he sits with Daddy.

Daddy yells, "I feel like a wing up here in the air."

"A bird, Daddy," Emmett says.

"That's right. That's the word." Daddy waves to the folks on the other chairlift coming down the mountain, and they wave back. I get a spinning sensation in my stomach the higher we get, and my ears start popping. I swear, it's like heading straight to the sky. I sit with Gentle and Caroline on either side of me, while Cyrus sits behind us in another chair between Jitters and Grandma Horace, a grin of pure joy on his face. Grandma Horace has got her eagle eye out for Uncle Buddy, and I don't envy him a minute when she gets her clutches into him.

Folks ride the double-incline railway running right alongside the chairlift up the mountain on little-bitty railroad tracks. In my opinion, the chairlift is the best way to go. The breeze on the mountain carries the smell of rain, cotton candy, and barbecue sauce. I'm faint with hunger, and if Emmett's got free passes for food, too, I hope to try a bite of every kind of food cooked up at Ghost Town.

As we get higher up the mountain, lightning bolts resemble white spiders in the sky, and booming claps of thunder pound from above, and I grip the handle of the chairlift. I've never been in a thunderstorm on a swinging chairlift before. The little ones start crying, so I hug them close and sing them an old song, "Soldier's Joy," from a bluegrass band Daddy used to love called the Skillet Lickers. Then, about five chairs ahead of us, there's a sudden commotion. A man lifts up the safety bar to his chair and yells, "By God, I'd rather take my chances jumping off than get struck by lightning. Geronimo!" The lady next to him hollers,

"You idiot! Fool! My husband! No!" as he plunges into the treetops below.

Emmett yells into the wind, "Don't worry! He'll be fine. Trees'll break his fall."

Folks on the ground commence to yelling along with the wife of the jumper as the storm whips up in a fury of rain, hail like rock salt cuts the air, and the wind bawls like a giant hound dog. Cyrus ducks under Grandma Horace's cardigan like a little bird. Jitters is trying to say something, but the wind snatches away her voice. The chairs knock back and forth as the chairlift creeps up the mountain. I need Louise. If she were here, she'd say, "Look, Livy Two, it's a Vincent van Gogh sky. All swirly and alive. Don't be scared." It's only folks that scare Louise, not storms or snakes.

Please let us get there, please let us get there. . . . I feel sick at my stomach like this might be the end. What if a tornado comes and whips us off the pulleys and sends us flying? At least the electricity is still working or else we'd all be sitting ducks. The incline train has already stopped at the top and let its travelers off. Near the exit of the ride, a pretty woman, dressed liked a blacksmith in a heavy leather apron, rushes around to help folks off, getting soaked herself. I wonder if this is the same blacksmith Emmett wrote about in his letter from Amish country.

When the ride finally comes to an end, Emmett flies off somewhere before I can ask him. More Ghost Town workers help us onto golf carts. They give us blankets and drive us up to the Silver Dollar Saloon on Main Street of the fake town for free cups of hot chocolate. The blacksmith lady greets us at the door. "Right this way now. Step inside and get warm. They got hot chocolate lined up on the bar. Get yourselves a cup. This way. Come on now." She hustles us all inside.

Grandma Horace gropes for a chair as the blacksmith lady pats her and says, "Are you all in one piece, ma'am?"

"Well, if I am it's certainly no thanks to Ghost Town's management! I am soaked to the skin!" Grandma Horace snarls, her gray glass eye placid, but her good eye full of the same fury as the stormy sky outside. "What about that poor half-wit who jumped?"

"Somebody'll fetch him, but he wasn't right in the head to do that."

Cyrus drinks his hot chocolate and says, "Maybe he thought he could fly?"

"Scared me with that terrible lightning so close to my grandchildren." Grandma Horace sips her hot chocolate, but the lady blacksmith says, "Wait a minute. Don't y'all folks know that fancy chairlift is lightning proof?"

"Never heard of such a thing!" says a man cleaning his wet spectacles.

"Well then . . ." The blacksmith speaks in a voice as smooth as honey. "It's a good thing I'm on my break to tell y'all folks the story. The boss of Ghost Town himself went clear to Italy to bring this chairlift back. You're safer on this chairlift in a thunderstorm than in your own home and that's the truth."

"That's right. Safer than in your own home!" Emmett repeats like he's heard it plenty as he strolls in the saloon, carrying a stack of towels. "Here you go. More towels to get dry! Mrs. Whelan, I'd like you to meet my family. Everybody, this is Mrs. Clare Whelan. She and her husband are the blacksmiths at Ghost Town."

Daddy nods at Mrs. Whelan but says, "What chairlift?"

Cyrus says, "Down there, Daddy. We just rode it, big silly."

Daddy looks embarrassed. "Is that a fact?"

Mrs. Whelan smiles at all of us. "Well, well, Emmett's family! And you're the daddy. It's good to see you feeling like your old self. You played a mean clawhammer banjo last year at Settlers Days. I'm kin to Ellie Ketteringly. Your duet partner."

Daddy drinks his hot chocolate. "Who's that?"

"He can't remember stuff so well," Caroline explains,

while I read a sign that says: SALOON RULES: NO CUSSIN',
NO HORSES IN SALOON, NO SLEEPING UNDER TABLES, USE
SPITTOONS, NO PINCHING OF DANCERS.

The other tourists compare notes from the chairlift
and tell Mrs. Whelan, who nods and clucks in sympathy,
all about it. "Thought I was a dead man for sure," and
"Saw my life zoom before me," and "Anybody see what
happened to the jumper? Poor feller. I'm a-walking
down the mountain on foot. Can't pay me to get back
on that thing."

Emmett whispers to me, "Ain't Mrs. Whelan pretty?
She's married and too old for me, but she bears a mighty
strong resemblance to Saturn Girl, if you ask me."

Although I know better, I bust out laughing. Seems
like my brother is in love with a lady blacksmith. His
face flames lobster red. "Aw, why do I tell you anything? You're a kid. You wouldn't know the first thing
about it." This makes me laugh harder. I can't wait to
tell Louise, but then I remember I'm still mad at her for
ditching us.

When the sun comes out, Becksie appears, dry as a bone,
bragging, "I got a ride all the way from my boss, who
didn't want me walking in the rain. Isn't that sweet?
They let me go early at the Pancake House so I could
come. Come on, twins—me and Jitters will watch you."

You too, Gentle." She looks at me. "We're taking them on the kiddie rides. You're in charge of Daddy, Livy Two! Don't lose him, I mean it."

"I know that! You don't have to tell me! Come on, Daddy!" I take him by the hand as Grandma Horace turns to Emmett and says, "First things first—where is your uncle Buddy?"

Emmett says, "Beats me. I got to go do something. Be right back, but make sure all of you watch the gunfights."

"Where are you going now?" I shout, but he's long gone, and Grandma Horace says, "I'm off to find my brother. If you see him first, tell him Sister Zilpah is on the warpath."

Daddy's face is pinched with fear at the crowd, and he keeps hanging back, but instead of getting mad at him, I keep his hand in mine and try to act like Louise by giving him details and pictures and facts. "There's a blacksmith shop, Two-Bit Motel, the Red Dog Saloon, Southern Railway, General Store, the old-time portraits place, a chapel, and the marshal's office."

A man drives the antique stagecoach, pulled by two tawny horses. "Giddy-up! Ride the old stagecoach! First stop, India. Next stop, China. Bring a sandwich."

I hold Daddy's hand as we move through the crowd, but there's so many folks, I don't know where to lay my eyes next. The bad guys are gathered on the roof of the bank while other criminals seem ready to bust out of the city jail. Why, there's even a little cemetery called Boot Hill. I read the funny names of the graves on Boot Hill to Daddy: "'Joe Lowe, He Drew Too Slow. RIP. Eighteen eighty-seven' and 'Here Lies Lester, Four Slugs and a Forty-Four. No Les, No More. Kilt eighteen eighty-one.' Isn't that funny, Daddy?"

"What?" he wants to know.

"These little fake tombstones."

"Where?"

"Here! Never mind."

Before the gunfight starts, we go down Main Street toward the old schoolhouse to peek inside, since I want to see what old-fashioned kids might have looked like a hundred years ago. Daddy says, "I'm tired. I'm wet. Why am I so wet?"

"We got caught in the rain. Now, Mama says you're to take it easy." I find him a bench to sit down on outside the schoolhouse. I look inside and find a pretend teacher and her statue students frozen in time in the classroom with lessons on the blackboard next to a pot-bellied stove. It gives me a queer feeling in my stomach to see a dummy teacher and her fake students setting there so dead-still at those old-fashioned desks, and as I lean in to look inside, it's almost like a cold hand touches the back of my neck, so I run back to Daddy breathless. "I felt a ghost back there, Daddy!"

"Not me!" He folds his arms across his chest.

The gunfight starts with the crack of three shots, so I pull him back up to his feet and say, "Come on!" but he walks real slow, taking everything in, and I know better than to rush and get him all riled up. We find a spot to watch the gunslingers, who start jumping from the roof of the bank while others break out of jail, shots exchanged. Daddy covers his ears, and I try to find Emmett, but he's not on the roof. As more shots fire, folks scream like they're seeing the real deal, and Daddy cries, "Too loud!"

"It's just pretend, Daddy. Pretend. It's all right."

He squeezes my hand tight, and I hold on. "It'll be over in a minute, I swear."

"Make it stop!" He begs me, but what can I do? One lady gets so excited she jumps into the fight, and her husband has to fish her out of the dust-up. Next, the marshal rides up on horseback ready to take action on the lawbreakers. "Ain't nobody messes with my town. Don't move and you won't get hurt."

But a young gunslinger jumps from the roof and yells, "Give me the money!" I know that voice. Emmett's got a bandana around his mouth and wears a cowboy hat.

"Look, Daddy, it's Emmett," I tell him, and Daddy stops crying and watches the rest of the show from behind a post. He clings to it like he won't ever let go.

"You sorry sidewinder!"

"Look out behind ye!"

"Draw!" *Bang, bang, bang, bang, bang, bang!*

"Watch that one. He's getting away."

And it's Emmett who grabs the money and gets away, jumping on the back of a horse and galloping off down the street.

"These two are dead as doornails. Somebody go get Digger."

And before long, Digger comes out of his shop that says, DIGGER'S UNDERTAKING PARLOR & USED BOOT STORE. Digger steps over the bodies on Main Street and says, "Dead, half-dead," as he pokes each one with his cane, and all the folks yell and scream their approval.

As the fight ends, I tug Daddy lose from the post and say, "Come on," and we head up toward Indian Village, where I can hear the powwows of dancing and drumming. "I'm sorry it scared you so bad, Daddy."

"It did."

"I know, but they were just playing. This whole place is one big pretend, okay?" We pass by the merry-go-round, where the twins and Gentle ride around and around. It's right next to Custard's Last Stand, and sticky kids with snow cones and cotton candy line up to wait their turn.

Then I hear a familiar voice behind us yell, "Well, looky here what the bear drug up the mountain." I'd know that voice anywhere. It's Uncle Buddy in the flesh, with his shiny bald head, wearing a live iguana named Pearl perched on his shoulders like a rich lady's mink stole. The iguana calls to mind a miniature dinosaur.

He grabs my leg just above my knee and yells, "Horse bite! Horse bite!" It tickles and hurts at the same time, but I won't give him the satisfaction of yelling, so all I say is, "Hey, Uncle Buddy. Remember my daddy? He's getting better now."

Uncle Buddy says, "Still alive and kicking, are you, Tom Weems? Talk about miracles. You get my bird-house I sent you? It was meant to be a get-well present!"

Daddy stares at Uncle Buddy as if trying to place him. Pearl sticks out her pink tongue at several tourist kids who are crowding around to touch her. They shriek with terror, and Uncle Buddy snarls at them, "Get back now, she'll tear your heads clean off."

The pack of kids run toward their folks because the truth is, Uncle Buddy looks even more scary than his spiny iguana. He laughs at the scattering kids and calls, "That's more like it." He turns back to me and Daddy.

"You see Emmett in the gunfight? That was real nice of management to let him play at it for y'all today."

"What's that mean?" I try to keep my voice polite, because he's a grown-up, but I already hate him for taking my brother's money. I recall what Miss Attickson said about "quiet lives of desperation," but it don't seem to apply to him. Uncle Buddy seems to be leading "a noisy life of accumulation"—meaning my brother's money.

"Emmett's usually cleaning toilets or running the merry-go-round or stacking up the dry ice in the Tilt House."

"I don't believe you. He's a gunslinger," I tell him.

"Not hardly, my little friend, but they let him pretend for the family today." The old man hacks his smoker's cough that sounds like a dirty brown laugh.

Daddy finally says, "Who are you? Do I know you?"

But right then Grandma Horace shows up and says, "I'll tell you who he is—my brother, who steals from his own nephew. I've been looking for you."

"Oh Lord, help us," Uncle Buddy says to Pearl.

"Well, somebody better help you, because I have no intention of doing so. And let me tell you, sir, birdhouses and walking sticks with Bible quotes do not absolve you of your sinning ways."

Uncle Buddy raises a fist to the sky. "That boy owes me for rent, food, and worldly advice, since nothing comes free in this world. I only took what was owed. A man's got to live. Why don't you act like my sister for once?"

"I'm your sister, not your savior, Buddy Horace." Grandma Horace shakes her head. "Yet again, you have chosen to show your true colors. Now, my other grandchildren are waiting at the Wagon Wheel. Let's go, Olivia, Tom. Buddy Horace, don't you dare bother coming around again unless you have money and apologies to spare."

We leave Uncle Buddy standing in the dirt. "Fine. Don't invite me to dine, Zilpah, old Miss Perfect. Me, your only brother—but I want my birdhouse back!" He hoofs off with Pearl, yelling, "Welcome to Ghost Town! Home of your Wild West Adventure!"

We head over to the Wagon Wheel for hot dogs, onion rings, and Coca-Colas—delicacies I've only tasted once or twice in my life, and they're even better than I recall. We crowd around a table and eat like there's no tomorrow. Emmett says, "Let's take Mama a funnel cake." He wraps it up and puts it into Grandma Horace's purse.

After supper, we walk down to the blacksmith shop, where Mrs. Whelan gives us what she calls "commemorative horseshoes" that say July 27, 1963 . . . Ghost Town in the Sky. She's etched our names onto each horseshoe, too, so we'll all have one and never forget the day. She lifts each smoldering horseshoe in a pair of iron tongs and sets it down to cool. That's when I ask her my question that's been bugging me all day. "Mrs. Whelan, is that Italian chairlift really lightning proof?"

She smiles at me and says, "Honey, here's how I see it. . . . I tell those tourists it is lightning proof to put their minds at ease. And if, God forbid, the chairlift ever does get struck by lightning, I don't reckon a one will be coming back to complain."

When we leave the blacksmith shop, we end the day at the Red Dog Saloon to hear some mountain music. A group of musicians stands onstage, playing "Better Luck Next Time" followed by "Eight More Miles to Louisville" and then "Barefoot Nellie." The crowd claps and stomps, having a high old time with the music. It feels like old times to be with Daddy, watching musicians pick and sing, but his face is a study. I can't tell what he's thinking or remembering. The stage is set up outside, so older folks sit on bales of hay, listening to the music, while younger ones dance.

For some reason, I look down at Daddy's foot, which is tapping in time to the music. I want to shout out this miracle sign, "Look at Daddy! Tapping his foot!" I find Emmett to show him, but he's already asked a pretty girl to dance, so I back away, watching him laugh with her as they two-step around the stage. The way that girl looks at him, you'd think he was the most good-looking boy alive. The twins and Gentle dance with each other, and Becksie starts clogging with Jitters, and folks clear a space because even Becksie's dancing demands attention, and Jitters is determined to keep up.

Then Uncle Buddy gets into the thick of it, clogging in perfect time to the music. I wonder where he has stowed Pearl. He clogs toward Grandma Horace, who ignores him when he invites her to dance with him.

I sit on the bale of hay, hugging my knees close. I look out over the mountains, where the July sky above Ghost Town resembles a bruised plum with flecks of gold light from the setting sun. Sometimes, I don't feel like a kid anymore.

Then one of the musicians onstage steps forward and says, "It's been called to my attention that we have a special guest in the house tonight. Mr. Tom Weems. Glad to see you're out and about again with us, Tom. Folks, Mr. Weems is a musician who judged Settlers Days last year down in Maggie, and we'd like to have his daughter, Olivia Hyatt Weems, come up and sing with us some of the songs she sang last year at the Mountain Dance and Folk Music Festival."

I get knots in my stomach and say, "I don't have my guitar. I ain't practiced."

"We got one, little girl! Heck, we got more than one! Don't be shy."

The audience claps, so I go up and get the guitar, which is a little big for me, and a buzzing roars in my ears like a slow-motion tidal wave. . . . My face feels red hot, but I find my voice and start with "Daddy's Roasted Peanuts," a song he always liked about roasted peanuts on a yellow crackling fire. Then I sing some more of the songs I sang last year over in Asheville, the night of Daddy's car wreck. He never got to hear me sing the songs, so I sing them for him now. The other musicians start playing along with me.

Suddenly, I hear Gentle singing along from Grandma Horace's lap, and next thing I know, Emmett lifts Gentle on the stage, and she stands next to me and joins me in singing more songs to Daddy too. Somebody gives her a microphone, and together we sing "Mama's Biscuits" and "Buttermilk Moon." Gentle knows all the words and sings them in a voice that is pure and clean and holy, just like Mama says it is. Emmett joins in on his harmonica, and I sing like I'll never quit, because it's only when I'm singing that I can quit hurting for Daddy and start loving him again the way I used to. When I look out at my daddy, Grandma Horace is patting his hand because he's crying.

CHAPTER SIXTEEN

Crooked Lady Scarecrow

EMMETT STAYS AT Ghost Town and promises not to be gone so long next time. Although it was a special day, the trip to Ghost Town wears Daddy out, leaving him with a bad headache. Mama rubs lavender on his temples and gives him aspirin, and this seems to ease the pain. Daddy asks for Emmett, looking around for him, so we have to keep explaining that Emmett lives up at Ghost Town, working as a jack-of-all-trades, but this explanation is not satisfactory. He stares out the smokehouse window as if he's looking for Emmett to come home. Daddy also has a hunger for blueberries these days, so we pick them for him and leave them in a bowl by his bedside every day. But Daddy don't call them blueberries . . . he calls them itty-bitty purple globes, and the little ones fight over who gets to bring Daddy his itty-bitty purple globes.

As for Louise, I want to tell her about Daddy's foot tapping to the music and him crying as me and Gentle sang, but she should have been there herself to see it. Besides, if she had come, I bet Daddy wouldn't have been near as scared during the gunfight. I'm not even going to tell her about the van Gogh sky from the chairlift or about Uncle Buddy's iguana, Pearl, or about Emmett, outlaw gunslinger, playing a version of Jesse James. For the time being, I am plain not speaking to Louise.

Late one night, something odd happens. I hear the typewriter from the smokehouse. A peck at a time. *Tap, tap, tap. Peck, peck. Tap. Peck. Tap, tap, tap.* Nobody else hears it, as they're all sound asleep, but this is a new sound from Daddy's living quarters. It goes on and on, and finally, after it quits, and I'm sure Daddy is asleep, I climb out of my window into the leaves of the red maple. I creep down the branches and cross the yard over to the smokehouse with the lantern to see what he's been typing. While he snores in his bed, I hold the lantern over the words on the onion-skin paper, the kind we buy 'cause it's the cheapest and comes in bulk. I read Daddy's words.

Dear Emmett,
I think I finally understand that you live at the night watchman cabin with that iguana man on top of the carni-

val mountain. Is this correct? Son, I don't understand how the words can find their way through my fingers to the keys of this machine to the paper, but not to my mouth. When I try to speak words into the air, it's like a hurricane in my head, but I discovered I can type. . . . I do not touch the banjo, though, and this distresses your sister to no end. I don't want to know if I can still play. My memory is pale clouds these days.

Your loving father, Tom

P.S. I'm hunting agates, pure perfect stones. I had some to give you, and I forgot. I forget a lot these days. The thought is there for a second and then is long gone. Are you going to live up on top of that carnival mountain forever? Why?

I can't hardly breathe, staring at the words. Daddy is in there. He's locked in his brain—he can't say the words out loud. I want to race into the house to wake up Mama to tell her, but at that moment, I hear crying from the garden. I peek out of the smokehouse window and see Mama, wearing her long white nightgown, barefoot, trying to make Stella, the crooked lady scarecrow with the wings, stand up straight. But the more she tries to stuff Stella with rags, the more fragile Stella becomes because Mama's too rough with her. The pie pans on the scarecrow's arms slap together in the darkness like pitiful cymbals; the wings don't much look like wings no more.

With one last push into the ground, the crooked lady scarecrow finally gives up and topples over on its side in a heap. Mama sits down next to Stella, her head in her arms, her shoulders shaking. I want to go to her, but Grandma Horace appears out of the darkness in her chenille bathrobe. Without a word, she steps over the marigolds and into the circle garden where Mama weeps. It takes some doing with her broad hips, but she gets down on the ground herself and sits next to Mama and holds out her arms. Mama cuddles up in those arms like she's nothing but a little kid and cries as if her heart is like to break.

The next morning, Mama is up making breakfast as usual. In the kitchen, the cornbread rises in the wood-stove, and the coffee brews. I rub my eyes awake at the table, wondering if last night was a dream. The only telltale signs are Mama's eyes, which are red with purple smudges of worry under each eye. I spoon bites of oatmeal into baby Tom-Bill's mouth, but I reach for Mama's hand with my free hand. It feels rough and calloused from how hard she works. With nobody else in the kitchen yet, I show Mama the letter from Daddy's typewriter.

She reads it carefully, but all she says is, "I know this

already. . . . Your daddy has written other letters, shorter ones, darling. And I'm very grateful he is slowly coming back to us, but I don't know how we're going to face the winter with him not yet working. Last night, I was speaking to your grandmother and she thinks—"

Grandma Horace comes into the kitchen and says, "My ears are burning. I can speak for myself." Two or three kids follow her underfoot. "Good morning, children. Well, who wants to drive with me over to Enka to have a nice talk with the school principal? Your mama and I came to some sound decisions last night, didn't we? A real heart-to-heart. I'm fit to bust that you have seen the light, Jessie. Now, I'll have to write a letter to Mr. and Mrs. J. T. Shelnutt, my renters, to tell them they'll need to find a new place to live. I'm sure we could have it all worked out in a few months, maybe before Christmas even."

Gentle plays the piano from the other room, picking out the tune to "You Are My Sunshine." Nobody says a word, but I feel a cold chill when Mama says, "Children, I've thought about it, and we'll be closer to Gentle's eye doctor, Daddy's doctors . . . I might even apply for a secretarial job at American Enka. Won't that be something?" Mama sounds like a robot, like somebody stole her brain.

Becksie stands in the doorway and shouts, "No! It

wouldn't be something at all. I'm the queen of Maggie School. I am not moving just when I got crowned."

Jitters, always the campaign manager, says in a tiny voice, "That's right, she's queen. You can't expect her to give up her crown to Evie Pepper. Please! That would be a terrible tragedy after we worked so hard."

I've lost my appetite for talk and breakfast, so I race out of the house and down the trail into the woods where I don't stop until I'm at the river, threading a red worm through the hook on my fishing pole that I keep in a hollow tree. Mountain trout like red worms best, and they're easy to dig up in the damp soil. The sunlight dances off the water through the canopy of trees. I step into the creek up to my knees and let the icy rivulets make me numb through and through. I toss in the line and wait for the fish to start biting.

It is only then that I allow myself to hear Grandma Horace's words of moving to Enka. I thought she was being sweet to Mama, holding her close, patting her head, but she was only tricking her into moving.

Grandma Horace takes the twins and Gentle over to Enka to have a nice chat with the principal of the school. Becksie and Jitters refuse to go along, not even when Grandma Horace tries to bribe everyone with fifty-cent ice-cream sundaes from Howdy-Do Mae's.

For once, we're all on the same side and won't be bought with scoops of ice cream. I desperately want to make a plan with Louise to put a stop to this bulldozer scheme, but she's with Ruth all the time now, no lie. It's like she's discovered a kindred spirit in Ruth, and that's how she distracts herself and lets herself forget—playing with Ruth and working with Daddy on his flashcards. We can't up and leave—how can we? All our stories that Louise painted are on the smokehouse walls. All our labor is blooming in the garden with the shucky beans sprouting up in the multitudes. We managed all right last winter with the root cellar. Sure it'll be hard, but Bony Birdy Sweetpea gives milk in all seasons, and I can chop a heap of wood for the woodstove.

A few days after the Enka announcement, I find Louise and Ruth together, *again*, in the back field putting the finishing touches on a fairy house for the little ones. Because Ruth is such a good carpenter, she and Louise built the entire skeleton of the fairy house the day we were at Ghost Town. Now they're carving tiny plates for the fairies, and a table and chairs too, and a staircase.

"Why would fairies need a fancy winding staircase?" I ask Ruth as she hammers a piece of plywood reinforcement to the fairy house.

"It was fun to make the steps out of little match-boxes." She uses her fingers to show me how a fairy might march up the play steps.

"But fairies fly," I argue. "What do they need to walk for?"

"Livy Two, just hush!" Louise paints a bouquet of sunflowers on the fairy house.

Ruth looks worried under her blue bonnet. "You don't like it?"

"It's just logical that fairies . . . forget it." If you have to explain everything, what's the point? Louise and Ruth go back to work, their heads together, connected with thoughts. It's more than I can stand. "Hey, Louise, what about the Uncle Hazard fairy tale we were going to write together?" I know I sound like a jealous fiend, but I don't care.

Louise says, "I didn't forget."

Ruth says, "You two are going to write fairy tales together?"

I say, "I'll write the words and Louise will paint the pictures. It's for the little ones. It's about wishes and adventures." *That is until* you *came along, girl!*

"What are some of the pictures?" Ruth asks.

"Lighthouses, oceans, killer whales," I say. "An Uncle Hazard fairy tale."

Ruth says, "Hey, I have an idea. What if you made the fairy tale pop up, say, three-dimensional shapes—so

Gentle could read them, too, with her fingers?"

And with this idea, my jealousy for Ruth starts to fade, because I think of Gentle's little fingers tracing the lighthouse, ocean, seeing the pictures for herself, using her fingers for eyes. And I also think of how good it is for Louise to have made a friend. I look at this Mennonite girl in her apron and bonnet, her head swimming with ideas too. "Ruth, would you help us make our fairy tale into a pop-up storybook?"

Ruth nods yes, and Louise smiles at her like she's the smartest girl in the whole world. I can tell that Louise hasn't said a word to Ruth about Enka-Stinka. She thinks by hiding from it, by not talking about it, it will never happen. But I know better.

When the fairy house is done, the twins and Gentle put little bits of crumbs and sugar and drops of honey onto each of the tiny fairy plates, so the fairies can have plenty of snacks, because, according to Caroline, you never know when a fairy is going to show up hungry.

Grandma Horace says, "That contraption stays outside. It will just attract ants."

"No, it won't!" Gentle insists. "This is for fairies. Not ants."

"Fairies love sweet things, Grandma Horace," Caroline explains. "Remember?"

"So do ants." Grandma Horace wipes Appelonia's

chin with a rag and sets her down in the playpen with wooden blocks and spoons.

But the fairy house attracts something more than fairies and ants soon enough. Early one morning, I catch Uncle Hazard slurping the sweet fairy plates clean like some grunting whistle pig, and I want to wake the whole house, yelling, "Wake up! Hurry! See for yourself. A wiener-dog fairy!" But I don't. Instead, I chase him off and say, "Uncle Hazard, those are fairy snacks. So quit it right now." He rolls over on his back, paws in the air, ears flat against his head, as if to say, *Forgive me.*

Daddy comes out of the smokehouse in his brown bathrobe.

"Morning, Daddy," I call. "Uncle Hazard's been eating up the fairies' food."

Daddy sits on the tree stump, rubbing his head. "Radio played all night long. Patsy Cline. Over and over and over."

"She died, Daddy, in a plane crash. You want me to mail your letter to Emmett?"

He squints at the sun sparking through the trees and says, "What letter is that?" I decide to mail the letter anyway. "Is Emmett coming home soon?"

The next day, when we're out weeding the garden and chasing off the crows, Louise says, "Livy Two, I never told you something, and it's been weighing on my mind."

"What?"

"That I'm sorry about Ghost Town—about the chairlift, the singing, the rain, the Cherokee dancers. Grandma Horace told me everything. Wish I'd been there."

"Your loss."

"I said sorry."

I can hear in her voice that she is contrite, so I seize the opportunity. "Well, how about making up for it by coming to Waynesville, then, to draw portraits for two dollars per person? Or do you intend to be shy the rest of your living, breathing life? We got to think of more ways to help Mama. Convince her there's other options than Enka."

"I can't just go up to strangers and say, 'Hey, want me to paint your picture?'" She waters the marigolds that have now bloomed fiery yellow orange, circling our round garden like the rings around Saturn.

"Louise, Grandma Horace wants Enka to happen. You know it. Do you want to live next to that stinky paper mill or that thread mill or tire mill or whatever it's called?"

"American Enka. It's a textile plant."

"Fine, a textile plant. But you heard Mama, saying

what it was like . . . waking up with that stench in your nose every day and getting to where you don't even notice it no more. Or do you want to smell honeysuckle, Joe Pye weed, snowball flowers, and sweet white violets? Which is it, Louisiana Weems? You want Daddy getting better here in Maggie or in Enka-Stinka?"

"Oh my Lord, fine! Just shut up about it."

"Fine, what?"

"Fine, I'll go draw folks' pictures in Waynesville if it'll make you happy. But I don't see how a few portraits are gonna do anything."

"Louise, it's all of us working. If we all stick together, we can do it . . . every little tiny bit. Mama needs us more than ever. There's still time to change her mind."

"But what am I supposed to draw with?"

"What's cheapest?"

"Graphite and charcoal, I reckon. But I like to draw stuff that don't talk back."

"Hold on a second," I tell her. I race over to the red maple and climb up to my secret box. I dig around inside and find the "1952 Greetings from Louisiana" postcard inside my book of E. E. Cummings poems. I run back over to Louise and say, "This is a secret, but I found it. If you tell, I'll be in such trouble, but I think it belongs to you. And you can't ask me a thing about it ever. Swear?"

"I swear."

I hand her the postcard and Louise reads Daddy's words to Mama, and her eyes fill up with tears. She looks up and says, "I won't lose it, and I won't tell."

Daddy calls from the smokehouse, "I'm so hungry I could eat a . . . a . . . a . . . something." So I go up to the back field to pick Daddy some itty-bitty purple globes.

On my way back to the smokehouse, I look out at the circle garden where Stella is back on the pole in the center, but her crooked lady scarecrow head is bent forward like she's whispering secrets to the cornstalks. I wonder who stuck her back on the pole.

CHAPTER SEVENTEEN

Louisiana's Song

THE AUGUST SUN bakes the sidewalk where Main Street is packed with shoppers and more filling stations than I've ever seen in my life. I count them as we drive through Waynesville. Nine! Nine filling stations. I guess folks need their gasoline whenever they please. Mama drives us through town, passing places like the roller-skating rink, police station, post office, hardware store, drugstore, Firestone Tires, Western Auto, and the Winn-Dixie too. Waynesville's a real town with folks everywhere. Daddy sits up front, since he and Mama are going to see the doctor to see how he is progressing. Mama pats his hand, and he smiles at her and says, "This is a fine car ride."

Louise holds her homemade easel on her knees, nervous as all get-out.

"Why don't we set up down on Frog Level?" she asks

me, which is the street below Main Street where the creek used to run over. She only wants to set up there since not near as many folks shop on Frog Level as they do on Main Street. I ignore this request as Mama pulls over at the curb behind a taxi stand. "Now, you stick together."

Daddy stares at all the hubbub of Saturday activity. "What the heck is this place?"

"Waynesville. It's the town closest to Maggie Valley, Tom," Mama tells him.

"I know that! Don't you think I know that?" He growls like some bear.

I whisper to Mama, "Why don't you if see that doctor has any grouch pills?"

Louise says, "Daddy, don't give Mama a hard time today. Be sweet."

Daddy gives a gruff nod and says, "All right."

Now how can she do that—get him to listen to her all civilized like that? It's a mystery. She's got the touch that I don't have. We watch them drive off, and I'm suddenly so glad to have the day with my sister in Waynesville, sketching portraits, making money, babysitting for no one! Hooray! I hope we make piles of cash. We did ask Ruth to come along with us, too, but Mathew the Mennonite said no, she was needed at home. Grandma Horace had to put in her two cents and swore it's because "street artists look like nothing more than panhandlers" and "Mathew the Mennonite knows best." She keeps talking about how wonderful and civilized life will be when we finally get to Enka. Since she only has a two-bedroom house, a bunch of us will have to sleep in the basement, and it's a fine room except when it floods. I act like she's speaking French or Chinese when she starts running at the mouth about Enka. At least Mama knows we're not panhandlers begging with a tin cup like hobos on a train.

But when we get set up on the sidewalk, Louise starts to get nervous. I pretend like I don't notice and put out a sign that reads JESSIE'S MOUNTAIN SWEATERS! $20.00 . . . A SMALL PRICE TO PAY FOR HIGH STYLE AND THE LONG WINTER! I thought it up myself, but it's such a hot day, I wonder if folks will even be wanting sweaters. Louise grips her sketchbook, waiting for a customer who wants a memory of his or her face forever. So far, no takers.

"Relax, Louise!"

"I am!"

"You look like a rocket about to explode to Mars or something."

"I wish certain people would quit commenting on how I look!"

"Well, certain people don't want to see you so worked up over nothing."

"This is a terrible idea! Your worst yet. Let's just sell sweaters and baby blankets and forget the rest. My fingers are too sweaty."

I don't answer for fear she'll take off running down Main Street. Instead, we watch folks load up on their supplies for the week like sugar and flour and eggs. Others mail their letters and stop to gossip about how this or that so and so was never much good and it's no surprise he lit off for Atlanta or Raleigh, leaving them all high and dry. One lady stops at Louise's easel and says, "You the Weems children? Your grandmother from Buncombe County has brought you to my church." It's a statement, not a question.

Louise mumbles a weak "Hello," while I say, "Yes, ma'am. How are you today? Would you like your picture sketched for your grandchildren? Portraits are two dollars."

"No, I would not. I do not have grandchildren, thank you very much. How is your dear father, bless his heart? Aren't y'all kids grateful that he is home and alive? Tell me, do you fall on your knees every night to give thanks?"

To be polite, we say, "Yes." The rest is too hard to explain.

"Well, I have my shopping to do. Tell your grandmother that Millie Rivers says hello, and we look forward to seeing you all at church again." She eyes Louise and says, "Aren't you a big, tall girl?" She marches off to do her shopping, and Louise slouches to look smaller, but it don't work.

Another hour drags by without a single sale, so to drum up business, I start calling out to folks like a carnival barker, "Portraits for two dollars! Two-dollar portraits. Only fifteen minutes a portrait or it's free! Come get your portrait done by a true mountain artist!" Louise hisses at me, "Hush!" but I ignore her. "Come on, folks! A lifetime keepsake for your kids and grandkids . . . sketched by an up-and-coming world-famous artist! We got homemade sweaters and baby blankets too. Sweaters cost twenty dollars, baby blankets, ten. It's a bargain, folks!"

Louise says, "If you don't quit it, I'm leaving."

"Like heck you are! We're making money today."

Before Louise can argue back, who should walk by but Mr. Pickle, who stops, sucking on a ginger drop, and says, "Well, look at the entrepreneur Weems sisters peddling their wares and talents. I had a fine time in Miami Beach. Did you enjoy the van Gogh book, Louisiana?"

Louise jerks a quick nod, and Mr. Pickle says, "I'm

glad. Now, I have zero interest in having my face memorialized, but I believe I might take one of these fine sweaters for my fiancée. She looks quite pretty in red." Mr. Pickle picks up the sweater, inspects it, and it seems to pass muster. "This should fit fine. Lovely work too."

"Our mama made it."

"Tell her it's beautiful. Here is twenty dollars." He hands me the money, and I put it in the tin box. "Red is a fine color for winter."

"Thank you, Mr. Pickle." I wrap up the sweater. "My sister has taught herself all the different shades of various colors, including red. Tell him, Louise."

Louise examines her fingertips. "Uh, cardinal, v-v-vermillion, russet, c-c-candy-apple red, um . . . scarlet, uh . . . blood, and brick, c-c-crimson, cherry, fire-engine, maroon—"

"Who is your fiancée?" I interrupt, wondering who in the world would stoop to marry Mr. Pickle.

He looks at me kind of funny before he replies, "Why, it's Miss Attickson. I thought she would have told you." He blows his nose to clear his sinuses.

A sliver of ice forms in my belly, but I keep my face blank. Miss Attickson is going to marry Mr. Pickle?

"Well, what do you have to say?" He gives us a smile.

"What's she doing that for?" I blurt out before I can stop the words.

Louise elbows me hard. "Livy Two! She, uh, means c-c-congratulations."

Mr. Pickle looks like he swallowed a lemon. "Yes, I can see exactly what your sister means, Louisiana."

But I'm too shocked by this news. "Is she still going to drive the bookmobile?"

Mr. Pickle says, "Olivia, do you think for a moment I could convince her not to drive the bookmobile? I only ask that she not drive when the snow gets too deep over Balsam. Now if you'll excuse me, I'll be late for my movie. Thank you for the sweater." He makes his way down the street to the Strand Movie Theatre, where the marquee reads: HUD . . . STARRING PAUL NEWMAN, PATRI- CIA NEAL, AND MELVYN DOUGLAS with a quote from the movie: "WHAT WE HAVE IS A FAILURE TO COMMUNICATE."

I feel breathless, like I might get sick, but Louise says, "It's all right, Livy Two. She's not dead. She's just get- ting married."

"But why to him?" Why didn't she tell me? But I don't have time to consider this much, because a pretty girl with long shining hair comes by and says, "Would you draw my picture, so I could send it to my boyfriend over in Vietnam? I think he'd like it."

An old man in overalls says, "Would you draw me and my bulldog next?"

"My sister will draw anything y'all want," I tell them,

and like I promise Louise, I do all the talking, so she only has to set there and draw folks, mouth shut. Soon, one after another, they start lining up, and Louise forgets to be scared when she's sketching. The pretty girl is followed by the man with his bulldog, and next she sketches a nervous kid, two lovebird teenagers, and twin boys, who have to be bribed with ice cream to sit still. The graphite and charcoal turn her fingers black. I sell two more of Mama's sweaters and three blue baby blankets to folks hoping for baby boys, and a pink one for a girl already born. We're not rich but it feels like we're on the way. Then who should walk by but our "filanthropist" friend, Miss Sweetness and Light herself, Evie Pepper. "Look at the Weems sisters. You're so cute with sweaters and sketches for sale."

I smile right back and say, "Why, thank you! Would you like Louise to sketch your face? Capture your youth and beauty with a few quick strokes."

Evie Pepper says, "No, but I'd be happy to make a donation to your cause."

"We're not asking for donations, Evie Pepper, thank you very much!" I tell her.

"I didn't mean to offend. Did I tell you that I'm going over to Edisto Island on Monday for a week? Tell Becksie hey. I hear she's practically living at the Pancake House now, working so hard!" She sails off down the street like the Queen of Sheba.

"I hope she gets gobbled up by a shark or a killer whale," I say, but before Louise can agree with me, Billy O'Connor and Rusty Frye sidle up from behind the general store building.

"Hey, it's the Tater Girls!"

"Draw me!"

"Me first!"

"Beat it!" I snarl at them.

They laugh and grin. "Come on, give us one for free, Amazon girl of the jungle. How tall are you now, anyway?"

Tears form in Louise's eyes, and I know each insult is an arrow in her heart. Those common criminals can't see the Louise I know—the one who paints her smokehouse art, teaches Daddy to remember things, who races through the mountains like a gazelle. No, they don't see that Louise. They only see the girl who trembles in fright, and then I can't take it no more. "Get lost or else," I warn them.

"Or else what?" Rusty and Billy shove each other, laughing and fake-punching. Louise's fingers are ebony with charcoal and graphite, but then she does something. She looks them straight in the eye, studying them in a different way—like they might be bugs under a microscope or some other type of unknown species. Then, without a word, she starts to sketch. At first I can't see what she's doing, but then I see she's drawing them like they're superheroes or something—a fact that could not be further from the truth.

"You want me to knock them into next week? 'Cause I will," I tell Louise.

"I'd like to see you try!" Billy O'Connor punches his hand with his fist.

"Yeah, try it! Knock us into next week." Rusty Frye thrusts out his puny bird chest, but Louise keeps right on drawing even when Rusty says, "We ain't paying you."

Billy O'Connor says, "Yeah, we're broke."

But Louise ignores them, her hand flying across the page in streaks of charcoal, faces coming to life beneath her fingers. Then she's done. "No charge." She hands them the paper. They both stare at the picture like they can't hardly believe it. She's made Rusty look like Lightning Lad and Billy look like Superman. It's clear they like it fine.

"Now clear out of here!" I tell them. "Scram!" And like that, the common criminals go off with their sketch. Billy O'Connor looks back over his shoulder and yells, "Thanks," but Rusty Frye keeps right on walking. Some folks will never learn manners.

Louise says, "Look here, I want you to stop fighting my fights."

"I didn't fight them."

"But you were going to. . . . I got to do it myself now. No more, understand me?"

"All right, I'll quit."

"Shake on it." I shake hands with her charcoal fingers.

We've got a long afternoon of portraits ahead and money to make to add to the "Deliver us from Enka" fund. I yell out, "Get your portraits. Done by an up-and-coming famous mountain artist. Fifteen minutes or it's free! Step right up, folks."

As I watch Louise sketch the people, I feel proud of her, and a song about her sweetness and shyness find its way into my head.

Louisiana's Song

If you call her Louisiana, she won't answer.
If you call her Louisiana, she won't look.
If you call her Louisiana Margaret Pansy Jeanne Marie
*   Weems,*
She'll never even hear you.
So please call my sister . . . just Louise.
She makes pictures come to life
Splashes of rose, emerald, and violet,
Charcoal and granite and cobalt,
A few strokes by her fingers,

She breathes life into her pictures.
She's my sister . . .
Louisiana Margaret Pansy Jeanne Marie Weems . . .
But please call her . . . just Louise.

I count our money at the end of the day. Twenty-eight dollars for Louise plus three of Mama's sweaters and four baby blankets too! Louise looks real pleased at her contribution to the Everything Box. One hundred twenty-eight dollars total! Make that one hundred twenty-seven dollars and forty cents after the two slices of chocolate pie we ate at Whitman's Bakery to celebrate after our long day.

Later that night when we get back home I dash off my new song and letter to Mr. George Flowers.

August 4, 1963
   Dear Mr. George Flowers,
   It is now August, more than a month since I wrote to you. Did you get the tape and letter and songs? I can't understand why I have not heard from you. Here is a brand-new song hot off the press called "Louisiana's Song." I await your reply.
   Sincerely, Olivia Hyatt Weems, daughter of Tom Weems
   P.S. I have more songs too.

CHAPTER EIGHTEEN

September Begins

AS THE MEAN yellow school bus arrives to collect us for the first day of school, Caroline and Cyrus board it, too, as they're starting up in the first grade. Pokey McPherson takes one look at their identical faces of freckles, and mutters, "Lord, Lord. I should have known there was more coming." Mama makes me and Louise ride the bus now, on account of protecting the twins from the mean boys, but Louise's tormentors have eased up ever since she sketched them as fake superheroes, though they still hold their noses when we get on the bus. At school, Caroline and Cyrus find us every chance they get, barreling like cannons into our arms at recess and lunchtime. Becksie, the Maggie Queen, joins the square-dancing club and starts up a public-speaking club, her two most favorite hobbies in the world. Jitters falls right in step behind the queen.

As for Gentle, she has to stay home with the babies and Mama, but Mama keeps Gentle knitting, and she also takes Gentle into the garden to teach her to water the plants. After her garden watering, Gentle works on the Braille alphabet. She can't read yet, but she's memorized the alphabet now. I've learned it by sight, so I can help her put together words when the time comes. Still, I see a hunger in Gentle's face when we go off, and she clings to us when we come home, wanting to know what school was like, begging the twins to tell her every detail of first grade. Uncle Hazard never leaves her side.

A letter arrives from Emmett, and I realize this will be the second fall he's not starting school with us. How can he have quit school so young? It seems like Ghost Town and working is all the education he wants right now. I take his letter up into the red maple and read every word.

September 1963
Ghost Town in the Sky
  Dear Livy Two,
    Thanks for sending Daddy's letter. I liked it. Did you hear about that big old train robbery over in England last month? They're calling it the greatest robbery ever . . . theifs made off with 2.3 million pounds, what they call their money over there . . . something like five million dollars in just

fifteen minutes. Uncle Buddy can't shut up about it.

I got a new plan, Livy Two. Maybe I'll go to Hollywood and audition for Bonanza *or* Gunsmoke. *I seen them on TV here, and I can do anything them cowboys can do. Then I could really send money home.*

Love, your brother, Emmett

P.S. You and Louise should work at Ghost Town next summer. That is, if you don't move to Enka! What can I say? I might be in Hollywood, but I'll still write. Here is some money for Mama. Tell her to put it in the Everything Box. Are y'all rich yet? You will be when I'm in Hollywood.

Gunsmoke? Bonanza? I've heard of those shows but never seen them. They got a television at school, but it's only to show special news programs or State of the Union addresses from John F. Kennedy. My brother is never coming home to live. He's got freedom for the first time in his life, and for him to come try to squeeze back into life in this holler or Enka might just make him fly to pieces. But Hollywood, California?

I give Mama Emmett's twenty dollars, and she puts it in a thick envelope inside the Everything Box. Since it's fall, Becksie just has a few shifts now at the Pancake House, but she still delivers all her tips and paycheck to Mama to deposit too. Mama's glad to have resourceful children, and no more is said about leaving for Enka or staying in Maggie Valley. But then a half-miracle, half-disaster happens. The folks renting Grandma Horace's house up and refuse to leave. They write her a note:

Dear Mrs. Zilpah Horace,

We met your good brother, Buddy Horace, up at Ghost Town. He told us that since the house is half his, he gets a say in the matter. He says we can stay if we send him half the rent. Is this all right with you? We are confused but truly want to keep renting your fine home, and we certainly can't leave anytime soon without plenty of due notice.

Sincerely, J. T. Shelnutt and his wife, Charlotte Shelnutt.

When Grandma Horace gets the letter, she about blows a gasket. I get scared that she really might have a heart attack or something. We pretend to be outraged for her sake, but we can't help being a little happy. It means we get to stay in Maggie until Grandma Horace can work things out with Mr. and Mrs. Shelnutt, who are "in dealings with the devil" as far as she's concerned. But she's not one to take things lying down, so she goes up to Ghost Town alone in the station wagon to speak to Uncle Buddy in person.

CHAPTER NINETEEN

Goose Boy

WHEN GRANDMA HORACE gets home, white-faced, she says, "I need to rest my weary, put-upon bones. Automobiles were not meant to be driven straight up that Buck Mountain. The vertigo got me so bad, I thought I was going to tip backwards. I need a tonic."

"Did you find Uncle Buddy?" Jitters asks, popping her knuckles with worry. "Did you let him have it?"

"I did find him, and he will be contacting the Shelnutts directly. Stealing money from the mouths of children. The Shelnutts will be vacating in January, so we are all moving to Enka come winter. There are a few details to work out, but that is the plan. Now I'm taking a nap, so keep yourselves occupied in silence."

With that, Grandma Horace goes off to rest, and nobody knows what to say. It was too short to be considered a miracle, but Becksie whispers, "I'm not going. I will not abandon my school or my crown. And you can take that to the bank, Grandma Zilpah Horace."

Even with school started, Miss Attickson agrees to let me keep working at the bookmobile two days a week until the first snowfall. As the days pass, I try to work up my courage to ask about her impending marriage to Mr. Pickle, but I don't know what to say. When I attempt to bust out with "Congratulations," the word gets stuck, and instead the words "Are you crazy?" want to pop out. So I keep my lips sealed and try to see the bright side. Maybe Mr. Pickle isn't too awful bad. He did lend Louise that van Gogh book that she studied all summer, but as a husband? Won't his stuffy sinuses get on her nerves? Will he whisk her away to Miami Beach, Florida, for vacations and never return?

On a Saturday in late September, me and Miss Attickson drive over to Dellwood and Cove Creek. At Cove Creek, a little girl brings us a jar of scuppernog jelly with fresh homemade bread from her granny, and it's about the best thing I've ever tasted. We steal bites of scuppernog sandwiches in between checking out books. Seems like we don't stop the whole day, what with folks wanting their books. During the late afternoon, I see the goose boy approach the truck. He's a boy with a withered leg from polio and a swayback spine, who limps along everywhere with his pet goose by his side. The goose waddles up to the bookmobile, carrying a satchel of books on its feathery back. The goose boy waves. "Howdy, Miss Attickson. Here's your Lord Byron and Elizabeth Barrett Browning back."

He takes the satchel off the goose's long neck, and Miss Attickson says, "How are you, Randal? Good to see you today. I have your E. E. Cummings poems right here."

I look again closer at him, surprised. "You like E. E. Cummings too?"

The goose boy looks up at me. "I am working my way through the poets alphabetically. I'm up to C." He gives me a big grin. I never noticed him up close before, and I figure he must be near my age.

"What's your favorite one of his?"

He shrugs. "I guess I like the one about the 'silver dawn' and the 'lame balloon man.' I also like 'Buffalo Bill's.'"

"Me too. I mean, 'Buffalo Bill's.' I don't know the others you said."

"You ought to know them if you like E. E. Cummings. Anyhow, thank you." He puts his E. E. Cummings in his satchel and loops it back over the goose's neck and onto its back. "What's your name?"

"Livy Two. I also like the 'angry candy' poem. Say,

what's your goose called?" I lean out the window to get a closer look, and Daddy's picture flutters out of my pocket.

"Clancy." The goose boy picks up my picture and studies it. "Who's this?"

"My daddy."

"I like his face." He hands me back the picture.

"Thank you." I sound stiff, I know. "Your goose sure is a big one."

"Talented too." Then we don't know what else to say, so the goose boy finally says, "Nice to meet you, Livy Two." He tips his hat and limps back down the road with Clancy at his side.

When the Cove Creek crowd clears out a little, I say to Miss Attickson, "That goose boy was nice."

"His name is Randal, Olivia."

"I mean Randal." I close the windows and shelve the books. As Miss Attickson revs up the motor, I say, "I have a question for you."

"What is it?" She puts the bus in gear.

I want to ask her about the nonsense of her getting married, and I want to tell about Enka-Stinka, but I'm too scared, so I say, "Me and Louise might make a fairy-tale book for the little ones. Do you think it's a stupid idea? Her painting and me writing? A present for Gentle's and the twins' birthdays. And Ruth, Mathew the Mennonite's girl, wants to help too. Make Louise's paintings into pop-up pictures in the book, for Gentle, so she can feel the mountains and ocean and fairies and all that."

"I think that's a fine idea," Miss Attickson says. "What kind of fairy tale?"

"An Uncle Hazard one. Our dog makes these adventure wishes that make all sorts of trouble for Maggie Valley. Mountain fairies grant his wishes."

Miss Attickson pulls onto the road and says, "That sounds fun. Why, you could even get the book Brailled for when Gentle is older and can read Braille."

"How?" I sit up high in the passenger seat.

"There are wonderful machines that read the printed word and make the pages into the Braille. Why, you three will be like the Brontë sisters. They lived over in Haworth, England, in Yorkshire, on the moors. Three sisters who collaborated and wrote stories together. Charlotte, Emily, and Anne. Oh, if I ever get to go to Yorkshire, I will have tea in a real teashop in Hayworth and walk along the cobblestone streets. I'll visit the old graveyard and climb out onto the moors to see where *Wuthering Heights* was written." Miss Attickson sighs as she brakes behind a stalled chicken truck.

I take a deep breath. "Maybe you can go there on your honeymoon."

Miss Attickson says, "I was wondering when you were going to get around to this subject. I love my red sweater from Leonard. Your mother is an artist with yarn."

"Leonard?" What a dumb name. *Leonard.* "Then it is true?"

"Does it upset you that much? Olivia, I'll be a married lady, but I'm not about to give up driving the bookmobile." She passes a little white Baptist church with a broken sign that says, NO MAN IS TALLER THAN WHEN HE IS ON HIS KNE S.

"Will I have to call you Mrs. Pickle?" I blink back the tears as I look out the window. The autumn mountains shimmer ruby red, saffron, and sweet maple.

"Would that be so terrible?" Miss Attickson's voice is tinged with sadness.

"No . . . I have something to tell you too. . . . My grandmother wants us to move with her to Enka when her house is ready. She's already gone over to talk to the principal. She wants us to go come winter because Daddy's not getting better fast enough to suit her even though he understands things more than we thought . . . on account of Louise quizzing him with flashcards."

"I'm so sorry." Miss Attickson's voice sounds shocked at this news.

"And to top it off, you're getting married. To Mr.

Pickle. You swear you won't tell him about Enka? Please? And you won't run away to Miami Beach, Florida, with him even if he tries to talk you into it?"

"Of course not. What an idea! And naturally I won't talk about Enka." Miss Attickson winds down the switchback roads where you meet yourself coming.

"Reckon the Brontë sisters' moors are like our mountains in the summer?"

"Yes, a little like our summer mountains." Then Miss Attickson drives me home to Maggie Valley, but I can't help but feel like she is going away on a long trip that will take her away for years and years. And what will happen if we really pack up and move to Enka-Stinka? What will happen to Gentle's Holler? My home is Maggie Valley. Miss Attickson understands my life without me having to say a word, but that could change, too, when she becomes a married lady. I love my job with her and all the places I'm getting to see as we drive through the hills and hollers of North Carolina—places like Crabtree, Cherokee, Bryson City, Fine's Creek, Bethel, and Canton, too, which has got the most lonesome bunch of railroad tracks you ever laid eyes on smack under an old bridge. Becksie says train tracks can't be lonesome, but how else do I explain the hollow feeling I get when I look on them?

CHAPTER TWENTY

Strike It Rich

A LETTER FROM Mr. George Flowers arrives, and Miss Attickson drops it off at school for me in the principal's office. I tear it open, and it is a form letter that says:

Dear Musician,
Thank you for your songs. Our office will be in touch if there is interest. We wish you all the best with your musical endeavors.
Sincerely,
George Flowers

But on the bottom is some actual handwriting from Mr. George Flowers himself.

"Miss Weems . . . Please give your daddy my best wishes.
George

P.S. Maybe we'll see you in Nashville one day when you're older. I liked the words to 'Louisiana's Song.'"

That's all I need to hear! I write him right back immediately.

Labor Day, 1963
   Dear Mr. George Flowers,
   Thank you for writing me back! "Louisiana's Song" is something I wrote for my sister! Glad you like it! I got more. I'll give my father your best wishes! Here is a new song called "Shades of Blue." I am very mature for my age, and I would love to see Nashville. I'm the head of the family now. Pretty much.
   Sincerely,
   Olivia Hyatt Weems
   P.S. Write back real soon!

I wait impatiently for Mr. George Flowers to write back. The money in the Everything Box keeps growing, so I ask Grandma Horace why we can't stay here in Maggie, since we're making ends meet and Uncle Buddy isn't going to take the rent from the Shelnutts.

"A drop in the bucket!" is her reply.

"More than a drop in the bucket," I tell her. "I'd say a few drops in the bucket."

"Don't sass me, child," she fires back, her hazel glass

222

eye fixed on me, fierce and accusing. "What with all the past due bills, back rent, and unforeseen future emergencies, we have to be prepared for anything."

"How do you know?" I ask her while she hangs ropes of beans, what we call "leather britches," out to dry on the front porch, so we'll have plenty of beans this winter to eat in Enka.

"If you don't believe me, take a gander out there in the smokehouse."

"But Daddy is getting better. You know he is." I pour extra birdseed in the birdhouse, so the birds won't think we're about to up and forget about them.

"Not fast enough to save this family from financial ruin and disaster. I've spent my entire nest egg on y'all, and it wasn't much of one to start with, Olivia."

At school, I avoid talking to Mr. Pickle as much as possible, but then he does something surprising. He commissions Louise to paint our mountains to give to Miss Attickson as a secret wedding present. The ice in my heart for him melts the tiniest bit. Maybe he won't be the great thief of Miss Attickson's life after all. He even supplies the oils and canvas for the painting, and it's the first time Louise has used oil paints, and she says it makes her feel like van Gogh. She paints out in the middle of the fields just like he did, letting the sun beat down on her, trying to capture Setzer Mountain. The wedding isn't until next summer, so she gets to take her time and paint some of it in the fall, winter, and spring. Mr. Pickle is paying her one hundred dollars, which I think makes us near millionaires, and I tell Grandma Horace, "Now we truly don't need to move. We're all bringing in money except for the little ones, and I bet they could learn to pick 'seng in the woods to sell at the Maggie store. I hear the herb is real good for sick folks."

"The little ones do not need to be traipsing off to Timbuktu to pick ginseng, Olivia." Grandma Horace calls it by its proper name, "ginseng," instead of "'seng," the way folks around here say it. "We got enough trouble keeping track of your daddy when he takes it in his head to go off roaming," Grandma Horace says. Daddy's taken a few more trips on his own to the Pancake House and to the filling station to watch the cars go by.

"But they sell bunches of it at the Maggie store, for headaches and toothaches and such. Anyhow, I bet we're earning as much money as Daddy used to, right?"

"Trust me, that is nothing to write home about!" Grandma Horace's hazel glass eye is fixed on the future, where life will come together with good sense, practicality, and the Methodist church.

"Why can't you learn to love Haywood County as much as Buncombe County?"

Grandma Horace says, "It's not a matter of loving one county over another."

"Then what?"

"Olivia, tell me, do these hand-to-mouth ventures of knitting, painting, bookmobiling, gunslinging, ginseng-picking, and waitressing come with Social Security? If your mama gets herself a job at American Enka or Champion Paper, then she'll have something steady and secure, and maybe they can find something for your daddy to do, too, when he's regained his wits."

"Daddy's going to play the banjo again. He just needs to remember how."

"Lord help this family that has been reared on false hopes and pipe dreams."

"Why don't you get a job at American Enka if you like it so much?"

Grandma Horace grabs my chin hard. "Child, I'm sixty-one years old, and I'm surprised that this year has not put me in my grave. This is not the life I chose, but I've embraced it because I am a good Christian woman who has earned her spot in heaven. But I still know how to wash out smart mouths with soap, so don't think I won't."

When Louise isn't painting Miss Attickson's wedding present, she and Ruth and me are working on the pop-up book of the Uncle Hazard fairy tale. Louise gives Ruth her tiny paintings for the book to make into pop-out sculptures for Gentle. Ruth glues each picture to balsam wood, which she cut out to fit the paintings. I write the story of Uncle Hazard in longhand 'cause no way could I ever type that much.

One afternoon, while we're working on the fairy tales, we hear more typing from the smokehouse. . . . *Tap, tap, tap, peck, tap, peck.* After it stops, I go out to see what Daddy has written. Daddy is curled up on the bed like a little kid, fast asleep, and in the typewriter is another letter to Emmett.

Dear Emmett,

Did I ever tell you about the chicken house we had when I was a boy? The old barn stunk to high heaven, and it was my job to wash it down. I truly hated that job, but it was mine. The chickens would get to squawking whenever they saw me coming with the bucket. I also had to gather the eggs. I have to wonder why the past seems so crystal clear, but the present is fog and wisps of blue smoke rising up out of the ground here in this holler.

I would like to give you an example of the clouds in my head. Sometimes, I can't tell all these children apart, Emmett. There are so many of them. One of them keeps quizzing me about the president of the United States. Is it FDR? How long have I been living in the smokehouse? I know it's a smokehouse because sometimes in my dreams, I smell the dried meat.

I do remember the prettiest agate stone I ever found was

full of white and purple rainbows. I used to get my bucket and go panning for emeralds and rubies in the mud up near Black Mountain. There was a place called STRIKE IT RICH *where you could sift through the mud in your bucket to find treasures. I never did find any, but I did like this purple agate. Every time you held it up to the sun, the light would hit it, and another rainbow would appear.*

Your loving father, Tom

I walk back outside to where Louise and Ruth work on the fairy tales.

"Who did he write to now?" Louise lies on her belly, painting a school of dolphins.

"Who do you think?" I secretly wish Daddy would write to me for once in his life.

Ruth carves the tails on a dolphin to match Louise's pictures. "Your daddy is getting better, Livy Two. I know it."

I sigh. "He sure is taking his sweet time about it. And we're the ones who are here with him, not Emmett. Emmett's living the sweet life at Ghost Town."

Ruth thinks about this for a moment. "Your daddy's memories of Emmett are the oldest. I think that's why he remembers him best."

Mathew the Mennonite pulls up in his black truck and honks the horn. He nods to me and Louise. "Hello, girls. Ruth, your sister and mother are wanting supper."

227

Ruth waves good-bye and says, "But your daddy is still getting better, no matter who writes he letters to. . . . I'm coming, Father."

As she goes off, Grandma Horace calls from the window. "She's a good girl that Ruth. Would you care to know the meaning of her name? It means 'friend' in Hebrew."

Louise says, "Then she has the perfect name."

I don't reply. I know Grandma Horace is trying to make up, but no thank you. I reach for my guitar off the tree stump and think of the chords to a song. It's inspired from reading Daddy's letter and arguing with that Buncombe County grandmother of mine.

Strike It Rich

If we could only strike it rich, we'd be happy.
If we could only strike it rich, we'd be satisfied.
If we could only strike it rich, life would be so sweet and
*   sunny,*
Instead of all the hours we cried. . . .

We deserve to strike it rich right this minute.
We're due a windfall of good fortune, yes we are!
If we could only strike it rich, we'd never have to worry
About packing up an Enka-bound car.

CHAPTER TWENTY-ONE

Alabama Girls

September 30, 1963

Dear Mr. George Flowers,

Something just occurred to me. Is Kitty Wells or Loretta Lynn in need of songs? Or do you know anyone that you are grooming to be a singer in need of songs? I miss Patsy Cline something awful since she died in that plane crash last March. Don't you?

Sincerely,

Olivia Hyatt Weems

On top of everything else, Mr. Pickle assigns me to do a report on John F. Kennedy. I study pictures of Caroline and John-John Kennedy in *LIFE* magazine at school, and it seems to me they live in a perfectly clean and shiny foreign country with clothes so perfect and so matching—no misspelled bags of charity for them from local do-gooders. So I do not know what to write about the Kennedy family. There is also the terrible news of a church bombing in Birmingham, Alabama, and Mr. Pickle makes copies of the story from the newspaper where four girls near my own age died. They were in the church basement, getting ready to sing in the choir, putting on lipstick . . . doing regular stuff that girls do.

I've memorized their names, because it makes my head pound when I think of girls my own age already gone without a chance for adventures yet: *Denise McNair, Addie Mae Collins, Cynthia Wesley, and Carole Robertson.*

I show the news clippings to Louise, and she can't stop looking at their faces either, because they're so young, and it don't seem possible they're dead. Louise sketches their faces, and one night after supper, I ask Mama, "Shouldn't we write President Kennedy a letter and say something? He lives up in that pretty White House with his children. Mr. Pickle says President Kennedy is real mad about the church bombings. Daddy always liked him and Martin Luther King. Maybe President Kennedy should go down to Birmingham and get things situated. Those girls are near our age, Mama."

"Lord, Livy Two, I feel real bad for their families, but I do not know what President Kennedy has in mind." She goes back to knitting her sweaters, rocking baby Tom-Bill's cradle with her foot in the front room. The little ones play Pick Up Sticks in the corner, but Appelonia keeps scooting across the sticks, so they have to start over.

"But what do you think, Mama? Tell me what you think. I need to know."

Mama sighs. "I think I've got all the events and folks I can handle right in my own backyard."

Becksie walks into the front room in her nightgown. "I smell like pancakes. Can't get the smell of pancakes out of my hair."

But I don't want to quit asking questions or listen to how Becksie's hair smells like pancakes. I want to talk to somebody about the Alabama girls—somebody who understands, so I find Daddy on the front porch. Maybe I could make him listen to me if I try. We used to talk all the time about civil rights and Martin Luther King and current events of the world. I fry up a pan of roasted peanuts on the stove on the porch, thinking maybe it will get him to smell things again. But he doesn't notice the peanuts sizzling in the pan even though it was once one of his favorite smells.

"Remember eating these?" I give him some salted peanuts in a cup.

"What?" He stares at the peanuts.

"You used to love these."

"Not me."

"Yes, you! Gave you song ideas."

"How about that?" He eats one.

"Your banjo must feel mighty neglected."

Daddy eats more peanuts without answering. I eat some too, but the Alabama girls swirl around in my head. So I make a decision. I pretend for a single moment that the car wreck never happened. I pretend the man beside me is the daddy I knew all my life. I'm sick of the words and phrases: recuperate, rehabilitation, heal, flashcards, lists, headaches, go find Daddy, where'd he walk off to this time, aspirin, turn off the radio, no banjo! I'm sick of waiting for the future that should have already got here by now.

"Daddy, did you hear about these Alabama girls? They died in a church basement, because they were black. Colored girls. Who would put a bomb in a church because of a person's skin color? You always said black or white don't matter. Remember, you said that? But a bomb? Where does that kind of lowdown meanness come from?"

"Meanness?" He rocks back and forth on the porch swing.

"You always said Martin Luther King was a fine man who fought for civil rights."

"I'm hungry."

"Eat your peanuts, Daddy."

"Where?"

"On your lap! Right in front of you." I swear I could almost smack him, but I take a deep breath and say, "Daddy, look here, I know you're in there from the letters you write to Emmett. Don't you miss us even a little? Do you only miss Emmett?"

He rubs his head. "Miss you?"

"Yes! Miss us. It's like your face is frozen . . . like you're living way on top of Waterrock Knob, and we're all the way down here. I'm trying to tell you something important about those Alabama girls."

"Where?" He looks at me sideways.

Then I can't take it. I just can't. Enough is enough. I start yelling at him loud. "I want you back the way you were! I want you back like the old Daddy. Now! Right now, no fooling!" I start crying and shaking him, but he says, "Not me! Leave off!"

"I won't leave off! Look at this picture." I show him the black-and-white photograph of himself that I always carry next to my heart. "Look at who you were. Look at you smiling and laughing in this picture. Look at it!"

Daddy studies the picture.

"Remember, Daddy? Remember?"

He hands me back the picture. "I don't know what you want, little girl."

"Call me 'Livy Two' or 'Magnolia Blossom Baby!' I know you're in there! I read the letters you write to Emmett. You're alive when you write him. Why do you write him with a clear head, but you act like Frankenstein stumbling around the holler with us?"

Mama marches out of the house and smacks my face. "That's enough! How dare you? Olivia. Apologize now. Right now. He's your daddy. He's your own father."

"I wish somebody would tell him that." I hold my hand to my cheek, the stinging red and raw beneath my fingers. It's like my cruel words are somehow tattooed on my face. I run inside the house with Mama calling, "Livy Two, come back here." But I won't go back and look at him or talk to her. No way.

I climb up into bed, but Louise is already under the covers. "Move over, hogging the whole bed!" *Will I ever be alone to cry?*

She tries to talk to me about Daddy getting better, little by little, and being patient, just loving him, but I've heard it too many times. And the truth of it is, Louise is just a plain better person than me. I'm so tired. "Louise, what are the shades of gray again?" I whisper in the darkness, feeling the grayness about to swallow me up.

"Charcoal, silver, slate, gunmetal, sooty, smoky. Others I can't remember."

I drift off to sleep. In my dream, I hear Patsy Cline

singing "Blue Moon of Kentucky" on the front porch of our old farmhouse in Tuxedo. It was before Grandma Horace was living with us or even speaking to us. Our place in Tuxedo used to be a church in the olden days, but it got rebuilt into a house. There's still an old church graveyard with four or five headstones left. It's overgrown with ferns, moss, and wild hyacinth. Nobody knows who was even buried there—some old-time family, I guess. Daddy heads out to the tree stump to work on his banjo songs. He is talking like he used to, not calling out the radio songs in his head. I yell out of the window: "You back to normal yet? Answer me."

But he don't answer. I race out of the house and down to him. Daddy is there, playing the same chords over and over to get them right. He looks at me and says, "Look at you. Growing up like a beanpole. More radiant by the day. You take after your sweet mama with that honey in your hair." He points at the row of pitiful headstones. "Livy Two, look yonder here at this little old cemetery. Would you take note of that old hackberry tree, growing straight out of the heart of one of the graves?"

I look at it, but I mostly keep my eyes glued on Daddy's face. "Are you all right now?" I ask him. "'Cause you look all right to me, Daddy."

"Course I am!" Daddy laughs. "What kind of question is that?"

"You're not mad at me?"

"Why would I be mad at you, darling? Get your guitar."

"It's time to eat!" Mama calls us to the table from the kitchen, and I can smell the steaming bowls of black-eyed peas with thick slices of cornbread. Smells so good—like home and food and folks.

I hang back and look at Daddy. "You coming in to supper?"

"I reckon I should, Livy Two, but you go on ahead now."

"I'm afraid if I leave, you'll quit talking again."

"I ain't never gonna stop talking to you, Livy Two. You know that."

"Supper! Now! Shake a leg!" Mama claps her hands and calls out the window. "And children, let's have some good manners at the table with plenty of 'please' and 'thank you' to spare. Hear me?"

"Please, Daddy? Come on inside with me. Please?" I pull on his arm.

But he's turned away from me and picks at the banjo, and I know if I leave him, he won't be there or he won't be the same. I want to memorize his face.

He says, "Are you still writing your songs?"

"Yes, Daddy, I'm still writing them," I say. And then I can't find him. . . . I only see the Alabama girls—

Denise McNair, Addie Mae Collins, Cynthia Wesley, and Carole Robertson—waving to me, smiling in their pretty church dresses. Then the real Frankenstein monster comes up out of the woods, stomping across the garden toward them, and I try to yell, "Look out! Look out!" But I'm drowning in sorghum, and the dream falls away into shivery broke pieces.

CHAPTER TWENTY-TWO
Fairy-Tale Birthday!

DADDY FORGETS THAT I called him "Franken-stein," but I don't. I carry my shame with me. I work at concentrating in school, but it's hard. I'd rather just write songs and fish and roam through the woods to soak up the last leaves of fall colors of yellow, raspberry, and marmalade. I talk to Livy One and say, *Please do something about Enka . . . don't make us go.* Some days, I almost feel her near me and other days, nothing. Some-how, walking deep in the woods makes me feel closer to Daddy, because he used to take us on fairy hunts all the time.

One night, Louise gives Daddy his banjo and she says, "Don't play it, just hold it. Just hold the neck of it and remember how it feels, Daddy. That's all."

We're all in the front room after supper, and we hold our breath watching Daddy clutch the banjo. He cradles it in his arms, resting it on his knees. His fingers touch the strings, but he doesn't play it. He seems content to just keep it in his arms. That's enough for me too. Daddy's hair is iron-gray now, and I recall how Mama used to dye it black for him, so he could keep up with the younger musicians.

I write another letter to Mr. George Flowers, so he won't forget me.

November 1, 1963
  Dear Mr. George Flowers,
  Here is another song, "Strike It Rich." Hope you like it.
  Sincerely,
  Olivia Hyatt Weems

Louise and I finish up the rest of the Uncle Hazard fairy tale about him becoming a brave lighthouse, and I start thinking up others to write and paint too. Mama agrees to let us celebrate the twins' birthday late and Gentle's early, so they can have their birthday cake and open the fairy tale together. And just like Ruth said she would, she fixes up the rest of the paintings into pop-up pictures, so Gentle can see them with her fingertips.

Finally, the day of the birthday party arrives. Becksie and Jitters go into the bedroom to practice clogging.

Their stomping makes the whole house shake, and the stack cakes tremble with the beat, yet the cakes themselves are towering works of art. Ruth helped Louise bake them, painting frosted fairies of icing to dance up and down the layers of the stack cake shaped like the Plott Balsams. There's dried apple and cinnamon filling in between each layer, and they even sculpted the bluffs of Waterrock Knob and made a waterfall out of icing swirling down the mountain of cake. Cyrus's cake is in the shape of King Tut's golden tomb, with King Tut grinning among his treasures. Mama let me keep my bookmobile money this week to splurge on the ingredients, and it feels like we're living high on the hog.

Mathew the Mennonite allows Ruth to come to the party, and she's so excited to see the little ones open up the pop-up fairy tale. After we sing "Happy Birthday," and the little ones blow out the candles, it seems a shame to cut into the chocolate sarcophagus and fairy stack cake. Cyrus can barely stand it, but he gets consoled by receiving the first piece of mummy cake, and of course, Caroline and Gentle get the first pieces of fairy cake. When we bring out the pop-up fairy tale and show them the Uncle Hazard story called "Lighthouse," the twins go wild, shouting, and Gentle reads the pictures with her fingers. Her fingers explore every inch of Louise's paintings and Ruth's carvings, and her face alights with smiles as she recognizes the pinecone palace and our house. "Read it, Livy Two! Read it!" she begs along with Caroline and Cyrus.

I start reading the fairy tale to the twins, but an unexpected knock bangs on the door, and out of the darkness, Emmett and Uncle Buddy appear, red-faced and cold from the November night. Uncle Buddy yells, "Heard about the party! Say hello to Pearl, kids." Pearl, the iguana, is wrapped around Uncle Buddy's neck, blinking at all the activity. "I have to wear her next to my skin or she gets cold."

Cyrus says, "Wow! Is she a dinosaur?"

"Close enough," Uncle Buddy says. "Keep back. She's an iguana."

"Can I pet her?" Caroline asks Uncle Buddy, and Gentle asks, "Me too?"

"No, y'all can't," he says. "Nothing personal. Pearl don't like to be petted."

"Why not?" Gentle wants to know.

"How come her back is so prickly?" Caroline asks.

"That's enough with the questions. Where's my sister? I come to bury the hatchet."

Grandma Horace says, "Well, you may have to do just that, but in my opinion, you'll never change, Buddy Horace. Now this is a party for the little ones, nothing more."

"Did y'all save us some birthday cake? Our feelings will be hurt if you didn't, I can promise you that!"

Uncle Buddy laughs, but Grandma Horace only presses her thin lips together.

Cyrus jumps on Emmett. "You came back again!"

"You think I could stay away? Happy birthday, little guy!" Then he hands out a present for all three, and the three of them tear into the box, and inside the box are fairy rocks every color under the sun. Emmett sits down with the kids and says, "From the fairies on Buck Mountain to you."

"They're so pretty!" Caroline squeals, and Gentle rubs them between her fingers. "What's this one?"

"Tennessee quartz." Emmett pulls Gentle onto his lap. "And here's a tiger's-eye."

Mama hugs Emmett and Uncle Buddy. "Well, get by the fire, warm yourselves."

Louise says, "Emmett, Uncle Buddy? This is my best friend, Ruth."

Emmett says, "Nice to meet you, Ruth," and he shakes her hand.

Uncle Buddy eyes Ruth. "Say, what are you wearing, kid?" He notes the apron and long blue dress. "Some old-fashioned costume?"

Ruth's face flames red, so I say, "Ruth is Mathew the Mennonite's daughter."

"A Mennonite?" Uncle Buddy whistles. "Never met one of them before."

"Now you have." I pick up baby Tom-Bill, who's starting to fuss.

Daddy studies Emmett and Uncle Buddy from under a birthday hat, and says slow-like, "Pull up a kid and sit down." Uncle Buddy chuckles, and Mama smiles too. *Pull up a kid and sit down.* Daddy's told a joke! His eyes feast on Emmett like he can't get enough. Can't Emmett see how much Daddy loves him being home?

I turn on the Grand Ole Opry station on the old Philco radio, and Becksie and Jitters clog together straight into the front room, kicking up dust. Uncle Hazard barks at their feet, and then Gentle joins Becksie, too, stomping her feet, swinging her arms above her head, clapping. Becksie grabs Gentle's hands, and they square-dance around the room, Gentle laughing and dancing like she hopes to never stop. The twins swing each other around the room, too, while Appelonia stands on her wobbly legs and toddles out into the middle of the cloggers. Even Uncle Buddy can't keep his feet still. "Hey, Zilpah!" He salutes her. "Come on and forgive me about the Shelnutts and our Enka house. I'm extending the olive branch here. I even brought you what you asked for. It's outside on the—"

"Never mind!" Grandma Horace carries in cups of coffee on a tray.

"It's a party!" I shout as I dance with baby Tom-Bill in my arms. "No Enka talk, please!"

"Sensitive subject." Uncle Buddy slices off a giant piece of fairy cake and watches the cloggers go to town. Then he says, "Hold up, I did bring a present. For Tom. A walking stick." He goes out on the porch and retrieves the walking stick for Daddy. "Made it myself. I didn't have time to carve a Bible quote on it, but it'll do the trick."

He hands the stick to Daddy, who stares at Emmett and says, "Will you stay?"

My brother blushes. "Aw, Daddy, I can't stay, but I'll be back again, I swear, like always. You ever hear of *Bonanza* or *Gunsmoke*, Daddy?"

Daddy grips his walking stick, but his face is sad. "How long?"

"How long what, Daddy?" Emmett's tone takes on an edge. The room gets quiet, and he looks embarrassed. "For the birthday party. I came home for the party."

"How many minutes?" Daddy asks, and Emmett's jaw tightens, but before he can answer Daddy, Louise whispers, "He does this. He asks questions 'cause he can't remember sometimes. It's not to make you feel bad, Emmett."

Daddy smiles at our brother, his face full of this bright happiness like they never had a fight in their lives, and they had plenty.

Emmett stares at the floor, ashamed, like he knows he should stick around more but can't. Cyrus climbs into his lap and says, "Want to read me some Saturn Girl and Bouncing Boy stories?"

"Yeah, sure thing." Emmett nods. "I picked up new ones the other day. This one's got Chameleon Boy, Star Boy, and Brainiac too."

Uncle Buddy slices himself another piece of birthday cake. "Ain't nobody gonna admire my fine walking stick? I swear, I don't know what a man has to do to get a 'thank you' out of some folks." His bald head gleams in the lamplight.

Grandma Horace says, "How are your teeth, Buddy?"

"Rotten." His smile shows gray, spiky teeth. "What can I say? Love my sweets!"

Emmett and Uncle Buddy spend the night after the party but leave early in the morning to get the company truck back up to Ghost Town. Mama also says Uncle Buddy and Emmett need to keep the rides oiled for the long winter and feed the horses that live up there, but I know it's because Emmett can't face another twenty questions from Daddy.

CHAPTER TWENTY-THREE
Waterrock Knob

THE TREES ARE bare once again like naked witch fingers scraping against the creamy sky. November 22, 1963, starts off like any other school day—better even, because Grandma Horace lets us eat the rest of the birthday cakes for breakfast and wash down the crumbs with milk from Bony Birdy Sweetpea. But when we leave the house for school, I notice a bunch of packing boxes piled high on the side of the porch, and my gut freezes. So that's what Uncle Buddy meant when he was talking to Grandma Horace. We didn't see them last night, because it was too dark. The evil move to Enka, North Carolina, stares us straight in the face. As we leave the house, Becksie walks over to the pile of boxes and kicks them all sky high, scattering them all over the yard. The queen has spoken with a mighty kick, and she doesn't turn around when Grandma Horace yells, "Rebecca,

I saw that! You get back here and straighten up these boxes now!" But we race to the bus stop like we can't wait to see Pokey and get on the road to school.

It all starts sometime after lunch when Mr. Pickle says, "I have terrible news. Please listen. President Kennedy has been shot in Dallas. We will all go into the lunch-room to watch the television."

The class is stunned. Is it a joke? A trick? Who would shoot the president? I mean, I know Abe Lincoln got shot, but that was a hundred years ago. Rusty Frye swears the Russians did it, which means we're going to be in-vaded any minute. "Will the Russians take over Maggie Valley?" Billy O'Connor asks, biting his lip.

We file into the lunchroom to watch the newscaster, Walter Cronkite, in silence on the big black-and-white TV. At first, Mr. Cronkite announces that the president is in serious condition, and then the word comes that he's dead. Mr. Cronkite starts crying on the television, and soon Mr. Pickle is crying, too, along with other teachers and students. Some folks start up praying, but nobody really knows what to do. A few kids snicker, but Evie Pepper faints and has to be carted off to the school nurse. One boy says, "My cousin just died, and nobody cried for him. He didn't get on TV for dying."

I don't talk to a soul. How can our president be shot?

He lives up there in that pretty White House with his pretty children and wife. I want to cry, but my eyes feel hot and itchy. I do not know what to do with my hands, so I stuff them in my pockets.

School is dismissed early and we are told to go home and be with our families. Pokey McPherson drives up in the mean yellow school bus, swearing up and down a string of evil words of what he'd like to do to that man in Dallas who shot our president, but then the bus is quiet for once. I hold the twins close on the bus and think about the Kennedy children, Caroline and John-John. They don't even have a father now, and all I want to do is get home to mine. For once I am glad about Pokey McPherson's lead foot as he speeds us toward home, fording the bus over the creek that has washed out part of the road.

Mama and Grandma Horace are inside next to the radio when we get home, rocking the babies. I can see their heads bent over the old Philco, listening in shock to the staticky news reports. They're too deep in their grief to even notice our footsteps, and they've got the radio turned up all the way. Gentle comes out of the house and says, "The president died. I heard it on the radio. Over and over and over."

From the window, I see the dirty dishes are on the

table, and a half-made bowl of cornbread batter sets there. An awful gloom has settled over the house, and the absolute last thing I want to do is go inside and listen to more news reports from Dallas. Appelonia toddles out to the porch, unattended, and I know it's because Mama and Grandma Horace are too busy listening to all the updates. Baby Tom-Bill sits on Mama's lap, playing with some of her knitting yarn. Both Mama and Grandma Horace are crying and holding hands.

I turn to the little ones coming up behind me from the bus stop. I whisper, "Let's not go in there. Let's do something else today. Remember that adventure, Gentle, I promised you ages ago? Up Waterrock Knob on a fairy hunt with Daddy? Twins, you too?"

They all nod their heads in unison, keeping quiet, but I shush them as they start jumping up and down.

Louise takes one look inside at the misery and blasting radio, and instantly, we're in agreement. "Hush!" she warns the little ones. "Not so loud. And we got to leave now without telling Mama or Grandma Horace. They'll only find a reason for us not to go."

Becksie says, "Well, I know what I'm going to do, and it's not going to be any fairy hunt, I'll tell you that much." She heads toward the empty boxes neatly stacked back up on the porch. She takes them out into the yard and tears them up with her bare hands. As she rips each one up, Becksie says, "President Kennedy is dead, and I am not leaving my school or my job at the Pancake House, so we are not moving to Enka."

Jitters watches Becksie, grim, tearing up boxes, and says, "Don't leave me here with her. I want to come with y'all too, please?"

Louise says, "I don't know. . . . Will you be brave?"

Jitters nods. "I promise to try to be brave. Can Daddy come too?"

Louise says, "Sure he can," and Jitters runs to get him.

I feel bad for Becksie, staying home to tear up boxes, so I say, "Are you sure you don't want to come too?"

Becksie shakes her head. "No, I got more important things to do than go traipsing off on fairy hunts."

"Will you watch Appelonia then?"

Becksie says, "Fine, give her to me. Now, Appy, you can help me tear up all the boxes, okay, sweetheart?"

Appelonia claps her hands and plays with the boxes next to Becksie.

"Hurry up!" Louise says, taking Gentle by the hand and motioning for the twins to follow. I scribble a quick note for Mama, so she won't be scared.

We're going on an adventure up Waterrock Knob. Remember how Daddy used to take us on fairy hunts? We'll

*be back for supper. Daddy's coming too. It's too sad a day to
sit still, Mama. Please understand. Love, Livy Two.*

I hand Becksie the note. "Will you give this to Mama
so she won't be scared?"

Becksie nods and puts the note in her pocket and
goes right back to destroying the Enka-Stinka boxes
with gusto. I look in the window and see Mama and
Grandma Horace haven't moved from the radio. I mo-
tion for the kids to follow, and I take Gentle by the
hand. She's got her cane, and everyone's got on their
sweaters and scarves, so we'll be plenty warm on the
hike up the mountain. I grab apples and raisins from
the root cellar, along with a jar of canned blackberries
and some potatoes, and put it all in a burlap sack. I want
to keep moving. If I sit still, I'll have to feel the loss of
President Kennedy, and I can't feel any more losses right
now. The mist rises around us and hangs in the thick
peaks above the trees, looking like lemon meringue
pies. Jitters brings Daddy out of the smokehouse with a
big smile on her face. He carries Uncle Buddy's walking
stick like he's been waiting for us to fetch him. "Hello
there, folks." He waves. "Where are we going?"

"Remember how you used to take us on fairy hunts,
Daddy?"

"Not me," Daddy says.

"Yes, you," Louise tells him. "Now, come on!"

Gentle tastes the air with her tongue. "It's silver out today, ain't it?" she whispers.

"Fairy-catching weather." Caroline skips through the wispy clouds.

"Wait! Can I bring Egyptian? My salamander loves me," Cyrus pleads.

"It's too far to carry Egyptian, Cyrus, but Uncle Hazard can come." I give a low whistle and Uncle Hazard slinks out of his pinecone palace, stretches, and flaps his ears—*flap, flap, flap, flappity-flap.*

"Wait!" Caroline shouts. "I need my fairy wings." She races over to the springhouse and grabs them off the hook on the wall.

And by nothing short of a miracle, we do not get caught as we sneak through the holler past the smoke-house with Daddy walking right along with us, practically leading the way. He hardly loses his balance anymore, and I can see his legs are stronger by how he walks sure-footed on the ground. Jitters hold his hand as we pass the garden where the crooked lady scarecrow flutters and flaps in the breeze.

"Hey, Stella!" Caroline calls to the scarecrow.

"Hey, Stella!" Gentle whispers.

Bony Birdy Sweetpea watches us leave without so much as a swish of her tail, and we follow the trail through the woods back down to Highway 19. We cross the empty road and cut through the field by the old silo barn to get to Campbell Creek. If we stick to the creek, it will lead us the back way up toward Fall Branch at the waterfalls and then on to Waterrock Knob, where folks say you can see everything for miles and miles including North Carolina, South Carolina, and East Tennessee. There's a topographical map in the bookmobile, and I have traced my fingers over the bumps and curves of the tiny mountain ranges on the map, so I'm pretty sure I know where to go. I like to imagine us as miniature folk scaling up and down the hills and valleys of that map. Dirty Britches Mountain is off to our left, and just over Waterrock Knob lies all of Jackson County. If we keep moving, we can forget this terrible day of losing John F. Kennedy. We will climb to the top of the mountain and show Daddy beauty and wake up his brain a little more, and maybe the little ones will find fairies or Cherokee Little People.

Daddy says, "Is Emmett coming?"

"No, Daddy. We're going up Waterrock Knob. He's over on Buck Mountain."

"Let's go there instead." Daddy gives us a big grin.

"You just saw him at the birthday party. Aren't you glad to be with us?"

Daddy says, "How long until we see Emmett again?"

Louise must see the flash of anger cross my face, because she says, "Our president died today, Daddy. Do you remember President Kennedy?"

"I remember President Roosevelt."

"No, not him."

"Then Truman?"

"John F. Kennedy," Louise tells him. "You liked him."

"I did? That's too bad."

I ignore him. I can't take his feeble brain not remembering even the most basic of information. It's been six months since he woke up. Six months. I wipe away the tears, because I will not cry. It does no good to cry. It doesn't change a thing. We keep walking, making good time, so we can climb to the top of the world and be home in time for supper. Caroline dances in the fog and cries, "Look! I bet hundreds of fairies will come out to play today." She chops at the ghostlike clouds with her fingers. She whispers something into Gentle's ear, and the two of them giggle together.

Cyrus leads the way with Uncle Hazard, carrying Emmett's old cardboard sword to fight off evil. He ties it to his waist with one of his mummy strips. He announces, "Uncle Hazard is my fair steed that never grew up! He's small, but he's still brave." Uncle Hazard barks and races back and forth herding us all together, stopping only to chase the red bird that flies over our heads now and again. "Let's find the Cherokee Little People, fair steed!"

Louise has got her sketchpad and colored pencils in her book bag. Jitters carries nothing but a worried frown. "How far is it again? Can we make it?" she asks.

Daddy says, "Yes, how far? How many minutes?"

But I just say, "Come on!" and we head away from Campbell Creek to a trail that goes up, up, up—so far up, it's hard to see exactly where it goes or if there even is a trail. We might have to invent one ourselves. Black slabs of rock and slate lead up to Fall Branch. We lie on our bellies and drink from the waterfall, the icy water soothing our throats. Daddy doesn't want to get flat on the ground, so Jitters cups water into her hands that he drinks up.

Thank goodness the twins and Gentle are too excited to feel tired, 'cause this is a lot of walking for little kids. It feels scary and wonderful at the same time to be on an adventure. I can almost hear the voices of the old-time mountain kids who surely hiked this way once upon a time. Maybe even the real Maggie of Maggie Valley had a picnic around here. Up in these mountains, it's like the meanness of the world don't exist.

An airplane flies overhead, and I wish I could join the pilot and go riding through the sky too. Nobody that I know has ever even been up inside an airplane before (except for Mr. Pickle when he goes to Miami Beach, Florida). I want to go places and see the world and do important things, but sometimes, it seems as if time is rushing by so fast, and I've barely done a thing. Maybe one day, I'll turn around, and it will be too late. The names of the Alabama girls come back to me like lost music notes: *Denise McNair, Addie Mae Collins, Cynthia Wesley, and Carole Robertson.* They were meant to do all kinds of things too, and they never got the chance 'cause of meanness and hate. A wave of panic comes over me, and I yell, "Hurry up, you kids! Come on, Daddy! We got a lot to see and do today before it's over."

On parts of the trail, water leaks out from rocks in skinny baby rivers, which makes the ground wet and slick, but we hold on tight to the little ones' hands and catch each other when someone stumbles onto the wet earth. Caroline wears her fairy wings, but they probably won't last the trip, as they're caked with mud now.

Caroline says, "My ears are popping."

"Mine too!" Gentle whispers. "It feels funny!"

Daddy says, "What is this place?"

"We're on the way up to Waterrock Knob," Louise tells him. "Now, be careful. Use your walking stick."

"I was in a car wreck, wasn't I?" Daddy asks.

"Yes, that's right," Jitters tell him, "and you're getting better."

But Daddy doesn't answer. He stops to inspect some moss on a rock and presses at the sponginess with his finger.

"Wouldn't it be great if you could turn your eyes around and look at your brain?" Cyrus's cheeks glow pink with excitement.

"When I look at my brain, I see mountains." Gentle feels her way up the rocks.

"How do you do that?" Cyrus wants to know.

Gentle says, "Inside my head is secrets piled up to fairy places."

Caroline nods. "Gentle is lucky 'cause her brain can see all the way to where the fairies live!"

Jitters says, "My Lord, I only got one normal brain and that's enough for me. Promise we won't get lost and become bear food?"

"We're not going to get lost!" Louise tells her. "Besides, the bears are hibernating now, and they don't like the taste of children."

"Are there caves up on the fairy mountain?" Cyrus asks.

"Nope, just bluffs," I tell him, "but you can crawl underneath the bluffs and rest and see just about everywhere. Now come on, we got a lot of ground to cover."

Caroline asks, "Are we on an adventure like in the Uncle Hazard story?"

Louise grabs her up and hugs her. "Why? Do you want to be?"

"Yes, I do," Caroline says. "I want to find the fairies who granted his wishes and thank them."

"You okay, Daddy?" I call to Daddy as he walks up ahead, leaning on Uncle Buddy's walking stick as he moves up the mountain.

"I'm hungry as a . . . as a . . . something."

"We'll eat soon. We'll have a picnic. I got food from the root cellar."

"I'm hungry as a . . . as a . . . something," he repeats.

We climb up the craggy rocks above Fall Branch, and I begin to get an odd feeling—like we're being followed. But each time I turn around real quick, nobody is there. I figure it must be my eyes playing tricks on me. Then a shadow appears and disappears in a flash. Uncle Hazard barks at everything, but maybe he hears something too. It takes about forever to climb the hills around Fall Branch, and we have to push the kids up to each level, but they hang on real good. I can't help noticing the footsteps, following close behind, and stopping whenever we rest to catch our breath.

The twins don't seem to hear it, and neither does Louise or Jitters, who climb ahead with the twins and help them beat the brambles away with sticks. But Gentle whispers, "I hear something." So I know I must not be imagining things.

Louise says, "Livy Two, how long you reckon it will take us to get up to the top?"

"I don't know, but let's stop at the next level spot, which will probably just have to be a big old rock."

When we find a bald that overlooks the Cherokee Valley, we spread out the lunch of raisins, apples, blackberries, and raw potatoes. Daddy sits up on the rock with Uncle Hazard. He gives bites of an apple to Uncle Hazard, who begs on his haunches for more.

I still can't shake the feeling that someone is watching us. Finally, I yell at a ring of trees, "I know you're in there. Might as well come out now!" It's a lie but maybe I can scare whoever it is into showing his face.

Silence—except for the rushing wind in the treetops.

Then Caroline says, "Is somebody there? Don't be shy."

Cyrus calls, "Are you a Cherokee Little Person wanting to play?"

Jitters buries her head on my lap, not wanting to see whoever it is, and Caroline whispers, "Maybe it's a bear," as we hear the crunch of sticks and leaves and footsteps. But it's not a bear at all. Instead, who should step out of a tangle of dog hobble and mountain laurel wearing her bonnet and apron but Ruth, smiling and waving.

Gentle says, "Ruth! You scared us!"

"How did you know it was me?" Ruth laughs.

Gentle replies, "I know your footstep and your smell—like homemade bread."

"I've never been so scared in my life!" Jitters cries. "I'm so glad it's only you."

The little ones crowd around Ruth, and Louise says, "You found us! How did you know?"

"I came over to your house and Becksie told me you were off messing with the fairies, so I just started running to catch up. I didn't mean to scare you. Father and Mother are home praying for the Kennedy family with my sister Sarah. But I didn't want to. . . . I wanted to find you."

Cyrus asks, "Was Becksie still tearing up Enka boxes?"

"She was down to the last one," Ruth replies.

Louise says, "Ruth, stay right there a second in the dog hobble like a princess. Don't move. It's perfect." And obediently, Ruth sits down in the ferns, so Louise can sketch her picture.

I ask her, "I don't guess you told your daddy you was coming, did you?"

Ruth shakes her head. "No, he would have said no."

"Just like our mama and grandma would have too." I give her an apple to eat.

Jitters peeks over the edge of the mountains and whispers, "I got butterflies hatched inside me. I feel dizzy."

"Don't look!" I tell her. "And you just think you're scared. You're not really."

"I'm not? I think I am 'cause we're so high up."

"No!" I lie, not feeling so sure myself. "Repeat: 'I am not a bit scared.' Just keep telling yourself that over and over, and you'll be fine."

"I am a not a bit scared," Jitters repeats as she peers at the valley yawning before us. "I don't think it's working."

"Hush, Jitters. You want to hear the song I've been thinking up ever since Emmett gave the little ones the fairy rocks? Take your mind off being afraid."

Jitters's face is white. "Yes, please."

"I don't have my guitar, so you'll just have to do with my singing," I warn her.

Louise keeps sketching a picture of Ruth, and says, "Sing to her, Livy Two, so she won't be so scared."

So I start singing a song called "Fairy Rocks" about Emmett's birthday present to the little ones.

Fairy Rocks

I wish I had pockets full of fairy rocks.
I'd build castles way up high—

Sapphires, emeralds, Tennessee quartz, tiger's-eyes.
Fairy rocks found in fairy forests—
Amethysts, rubies, garnets, jades.
Fairy rocks for fairy children hidden in a cave.
I wish I had pockets full of fairy rocks.
I'd build castles up to the sky—
Sapphires, emeralds, Tennessee quartz, tiger's-eyes.
Fairy rocks found in fairy forests—
Amethysts, rubies, garnets, jades.
Fairy rocks for fairy children hidden in a cave.

Jitters smiles and says, "That's pretty. Sing it again."

And so I do, and everyone starts in singing about fairy rocks, and when we're done, Gentle turns her face to the sun and says, "The wind sounds different up here."

"I like that song, but my legs feel rubbery." Cyrus eats his raisins.

"How much farther?" Caroline stands on a rock in the mist. "Hey, I think I saw one! I saw a fairy flying there! She's floating, not flying . . . floating on the wind."

"Where?" Cyrus peeks his head over Gentle's shoulder.

Gentle says, "I felt wings on my face like bits of lace." And whether it's the sun shining in my eyes or the joy in their voices, I want it to be real for Caroline, Cyrus, and Gentle. I want the mountain fairies to come and wash away the meanness of this day. I want to feel like a little kid on an adventure the way I used to with Daddy. I remember the first fairy hunt he ever took us on before the twins and Gentle were born, and even Jitters too. I rode high on his shoulders, and Mama helped Louise along. Emmett and Becksie fought over who got to be first as we climbed up a ridge toward some pointy mountains called the Chimney Tops over in Tennessee. Daddy said the Cherokees named them "Chimney Tops" for the way they looked like stacks of chimneys rising up out of clouds of blue smoke. On the trail up to the top, I saw a fairy flit above some Joe-Pye weed and touch-me-nots. Daddy saw it too.

"Did you see it, Magnolia Blossom Baby? Go catch it!" He set me down on the ground, and I raced up the trail after it, but Daddy yelled, "Almost, she's waving to you!"

"Where? Where is she, Daddy?"

"I saw her fly into those yellow buckeye trees. Next time." He grabbed me up on his shoulders, and we walked the whole way to the very top of those Chimneys, but my eyes were glued to the trail, waiting, hoping. I must have been four or five years old at the time. Daddy sang "Ole Mountain Dew," and we sang with him, our voices echoing across the mountains. Later, we had a picnic by some baby waterfalls, and Mama and Daddy let us wade in the creek for hours.

As he fished Becksie and Emmett out of the water to dry off, he said, "Hell, Jessie, I don't know how I got so lucky, but we got us the finest bunch of kids. Nobody can say that Tom Weems is not a rich man. Look at our kids!"

Mama was putting things away in the picnic basket, but she looked up and smiled at each of us, dripping wet, and said, "They'll do."

Ruth shields her eyes from the sun, her lips stained with blackberry juice. "You really going all the way up to the top?"

"All the way up to Waterrock Knob," Caroline tells her.

"You been up there before?" Cyrus asks Ruth.

"Lots of times for Sunday picnics. My parents love it up here. See that laurel?" We look to where she's pointing, at the green plant hanging from the rocks. "Father says when the laurel hangs like a giant's finger, it's not that cold, but when it curls up tight, you'd better believe it's cold."

"What's it doing now?" Gentle asks. "Let me feel." And so Ruth gets up and guides Gentle's fingers along the laurel that looks like it's starting to curl up.

"Wait! I wasn't done sketching you," Louise says.

Ruth says, "We got to hurry if we're going all the way up there and back again. I know these trails, and it gets dark fast."

"Where's Uncle Hazard?" Caroline looks around. "Uncle Hazard!"

Louise says, "Up yonder with Daddy on the rock. Come on, Uncle Hazard. Here boy! Daddy, you ready to keep going?"

But as we turn to the rock where Daddy was eating, he is not there. In fact, he's nowhere at all. Neither is Uncle Hazard. They both seem to have vanished in the layers of mist.

CHAPTER TWENTY-FOUR

Sisters' Journey

WE START CALLING, "Daddy! Daddy! Uncle Hazard! Uncle Hazard!" But no answer. A dread comes over me. The little ones start crying. I go weak in my legs. We're too high up into the mountains for Daddy to take off roaming somewhere even if Uncle Hazard is with him. I should have been watching, but Ruth came, Jitters got scared, and I started remembering old times . . . and I forgot . . . I plain forgot. *Daddy!*

"Daddy! Daddy! Uncle Hazard! Uncle Hazard!" Louise calls, and then gives one of her piercing whistles that echos across the mountains.

"Where did they go, Livy Two?" Caroline tugs at me.

I pace back and forth on the bald. "I got to think, I got to think."

"We have to hurry and find them!" Jitters starts crying in earnest now. "Grandma Horace will be so spitting mad at us, so mad . . . and Mama and Becksie and Mr. Pickle and the police and the army and the navy and—"

"That's a lot of folks," Cyrus agrees.

I can't breathe, much as I try to catch my breath. I was in such a fired-up hurry to forget today or make it turn out different. Louise whistles another ear-shattering whistle for Uncle Hazard to come on back. No luck. It's my fault. Because all along I've been so mad at Daddy, calling him Frankenstein. Nobody did this but me, and I can't stand it. I can't think right. I pace and start babbling, "Maybe we should go up, or no! Let's backtrack down. Or how about y'all go one way, and we'll head another. Or maybe—"

It's more than Louise can stomach, and so she grabs hold of my shoulders and says in a steady voice, "You stop it right now, Olivia Hyatt Weems. We're going to find Daddy, but not if we go six ways to Sunday, and I mean it."

Louise's eyes burn with gumption, and I got no choice but to listen. How did Louise get brave? I'm the one in the family who makes the decisions, but I'm relieved to let her do it for once. "But what if we don't find him? What if he is lost forever?" My stomach flip-flops. "Mama will never—"

"Livy Two, quit! You're scaring the little ones."

I glance at Gentle, Caroline, and Cyrus, who sit huddled together quiet as church mice on the rock, listening to every word. Her lips are moving fast and furious, but all I can think of is: *When did my dreamy, terrified sister become brave? When did I become so scared? Did we switch?*

Ruth says, "I remember a shortcut to the main road. It's not far. I'll take the little ones to the road, and we'll walk. I know the way."

Before me or Louise can answer, Jitters steps forward, and her voice, quavering, says, "Me and Ruth can do it together. We'll take Cyrus, Caroline, and Gentle with us."

Me and Louise look at each other, and Ruth sees our hesitation. "That's right. We'll find the road together—that way you both can go find your daddy and Uncle Hazard without wasting a single second."

Caroline whispers, "I want to go home. Let's go home, please."

Gentle cries, "I want my daddy."

Cyrus stands up and vows, "I'll be brave. You two be brave too. We'll be like the Cherokee who ain't scared of nothing!"

Jitters says, "I know what you're thinking, but I'm ten years old, and Ruth is eleven. That's twenty-one years between us, and we can do it. So go on! Hurry! Go find

Daddy and Uncle Hazard right now. We'll meet you at home."

Me and Louise take off running down the side of the mountain where we suspect Daddy might have headed. All those months of running instead of taking the mean yellow school bus have paid off, and we're flying down the trail. We keep calling, "Daddy! Uncle Hazard! Where are you?" We run for miles, it seems, as the sun sinks lower into the sky, shooting rays of primrose across the Smoky Mountains. "Daddy! Uncle Hazard!"

I follow Louise, never losing sight of her even as the sky grows dark. I touch the photograph of the young daddy that I carry next to my heart. *Please, Livy One, bring us to Daddy. . . . I promise I'll be more patient. I won't get mad at him.* The trail grows thicker with brambles, and I sniff the wet earth of night. It feels like several hours have passed already. The moon rises high in the sky, and a hound dog howls from far away. A flutter of wings crashes above us in the trees, but I can't tell if it's a bat or an owl. This whole night gives me sharp, slicing pains deep in my belly. I search for the Seven Sisters, but then I remember a Cherokee legend Daddy told us a long time ago that instead of seven sisters, the stars were really six brothers and a seventh brother fell back down to earth so hard that he went underground but then grew up to be a tree that shot up real tall so he could reach his six brother stars in the sky. *I'll help Daddy play the banjo again and remember things better. I'll move to Enka if that's what I'm supposed to do. . . .*

We come up to another path, and suddenly we hear a kind of snuffling, grunting sound. As I turn to look, I see a short, snub-nosed creature baring its teeth at us, circling us, growling. Louise whispers, "Badger!"

The badger stops and lashes out at us with a vicious snarl. The weasely body has a thick, short tail and black stripes across its face. He roars with yellow glistening teeth, ready to attack and tear us to shreds with those long front claws. My heart slams in my chest and I take a step backwards, but Louise says, "Don't move."

But at that second, it lunges toward us, and Louise grabs a stick up off the ground and screams, waving the stick at the creature. It ducks the stick and gives a few more warning growls before it disappears into the shadows behind us. As soon as it's gone, we start running all over again without looking back once through the smoky clouds starting to blow in like a giant bowl of pearly white soup, and I swear it's almost as if I can see dancing figures in the mist.

We race through bluish whorls and scrapes of trees bending in the crying winds until we come upon a road that looks familiar, and I can't figure out why, but then

I realize we're not far from Pokey McPherson's shotgun shack. I remember it from when we delivered *National Geographic* magazines last summer. We run up the road a mile or so, and the shotgun shack comes into view. A loop of smoke curls out of the chimney, and I see the mean yellow school bus parked si-goggling in the yard next to the house.

"Is he supposed to keep the school bus like that?" Louise asks

"Maybe he forgot to take it back to the bus yard because of everything today."

I'm not sure what to do next. Do we keep looking for Daddy even though it's dark, and Mama will surely be calling the sheriff if she hasn't already? But then, without a moment's hesitation, Louise walks straight up to Pokey McPherson's door.

"What are you doing?" I hiss at her.

"Hush, Livy Two!"

"I guess you think you're so brave, fighting badgers, that you can take Pokey on too? He might get out his shotgun or something."

"I'm seeing if he has a telephone. We need to call Mama and make sure Jitters and Ruth got the little ones home safe." She starts knocking hard on the front door. "Then we can keep looking for Daddy, all right?"

The door opens with a crack, and it's Billy O'Connor

again, who pokes his head out and calls back to someone inside, "They're here," like they were expecting us
or something. Louise motions me to follow her, and
I step inside the shack, and there, setting at the table
big as life, are Daddy and Pokey McPherson. Daddy is
holding the banjo, playing a chord. Pokey McPherson
says, "No, not like that. The other way."

My knees buckle beneath me with relief, and I sag to
the floor, breathing hard. I want to bust out crying, but
I don't. Not here. Still, I've never been so happy to see
someone in all my life. Louise pulls me back up beside
her, and we lean into each other. We can't take our eyes
off the miracle of Daddy sitting at Pokey's table.

Pokey takes the banjo from Daddy and plays a few
chords and hands the banjo back to him, and Daddy
tries again. It doesn't quite work, but it's almost a chord.
His fingers are stiff and clumsy on the strings, but he's
at least trying.

Pokey doesn't glance our way. "Now, listen, Mr.
Weems. Look what you're doin' with your fingers. Try
this. Like I told you. I wasn't never near as good as you,
but I watched my papaw play the banjo, so I know a
thing or two."

Pokey plays an A chord, and he hands the banjo back
to Daddy. Daddy plays it just right this time, and the
sound of him playing banjo makes me and Louise grab

hands and hold on tight just to listen. He plays the same chord over and over again. It's been so long since he's made music. I look over to the bed where Uncle Hazard is curled up, wagging his tail when he sees us. His belly looks full like he just had supper.

Billy puts more wood on the fire, and the little room glows with warmth. "Your daddy and dog showed up a while ago. Figured you'uns wasn't too far behind."

Pokey McPherson turns to greet us and says, "Well now, if it isn't my favorite Haywood County bus passengers. Olivia and Louisiana Weems. I was just telling your daddy a thing or two about certain conduct on the bus, present company included."

Louise touches Daddy's arm and asks, "You all right?"

But Daddy is focused on the banjo. He plays the A chord again, stronger this time. Then he says, "I took a walk. Me and that dog over there on the bed took a walk through the mountains and found this place."

We watch as Pokey pours Daddy some coffee and says, "I told him I heard all about his car wreck last year, and how I knew all about his bullheaded children, but that we all got our crosses to bear. Then I asked him what great man died today, didn't I?"

"Our president." Daddy plays an F chord now, not hearing how Pokey just insulted us.

"What's his name?" Pokey asks Daddy.

Daddy considers this a moment. "I wish I could tell you."

Louise whispers, "Look at this place."

I turn my attention to the walls of Pokey McPherson's shotgun shack. Every bit of space is covered with *National Geographic* pictures cut out and taped to the walls. There's the beaches of Malaysia, and the mountains of Indonesia . . . some statues that say "Terra-Cotta Soldiers in Xi'an, China" . . . monsoon season in India . . . and the Golden Gate Bridge of California . . . pure ice of the North Pole, or maybe it's the South Pole . . . a swirl of lights with the headline "Aurora Borealis." The Empire State Building in New York City sits next to shirtless African women holding babies, wearing big earrings and layers upon layers of necklaces that stretch their necks out long and lean. There is not an inch that is not covered with some corner of the world from all those *National Geographic* magazines. I see something else and say, "Look!" Louise is already looking, and it's the superhero picture she sketched of Rusty and Billy that day in Waynesville last August. Billy's face turns red when he sees what we've found. "Rusty gave it to me to keep." He rocks back and forth on his heels.

"You live here all the time now?" I ask him.

Billy nods. "My uncle don't mind me staying. Don't tell nobody, please?"

"Why not?" I ask him, but he twists away and warns, "Just don't, all right?" He turns to Louise. "You hungry? We got hoppin' John."

Louise says, "No, but do you have a telephone? We have to—"

Pokey says, "Bet your mama thinks the wolves or panthers got you. Phone's in the back."

While Louise calls Mama to tell her we're okay, Daddy plays another chord on the banjo. He looks at me and asks, "I used to play this thing?"

"All the time," I tell him. "You taught me how to play the guitar. You made me play at that festival last year. Louise painted the smokehouse for you to make you remember."

Louise comes back in the room, white-faced, shaking. "Grandma Horace answered the phone." That's all she needs to say as far as I'm concerned. Louise rubs on her ear like she's gone a little deaf on one side. "Mama is coming. She's on her way."

"The kids?" I ask.

Louise nods. "Mathew the Mennonite picked them all up on the road, mad as the dickens too. That's all I got before Grandma Horace grabbed the phone back from Jitters."

"Don't blame those poor ladies in the least." Pokey shakes his head in disgust, which makes me want to smack him one. Maybe he gave Daddy a place to keep warm and a banjo to play, but I don't have to like him.

Daddy searches our faces and says, "I want to remember."

I take out the black-and-white photograph of Daddy and put it on the table in front of him, so he can see it plain and clear. He studies it a long time, and so do Louise and Pokey. Billy O'Connor gets a good look at it too. Me and Louise sit down at the table on each side of Daddy. We eat plates of hoppin' John and wait for Mama to fetch us home. I put the picture back in my pocket.

Not more than fifteen minutes later, Grandma Horace's station wagon screeches up outside, followed by frantic footsteps. The front door bangs open, and Mama steps inside the doorway of the shotgun shack, wearing Daddy's old coat and boots like she's been out walking for hours. Her honey hair is wild, her eyes red. But when she sees us staring at her in fear, waiting for the fireworks, she staggers for a split second, trying to regain her balance. Then she says, "Livy Two, Louise . . . I've been looking for you."

"You got your hands full with them two, ma'am," Pokey says with a nod. "Bless your heart."

Daddy looks up from the table at Mama and says, "Jessie."

Mama smiles at Daddy and says, "Tom, I'm very happy to see you. I guess y'all had yourselves an adventure today."

Louise says, "Mama, we're sorry."

I say, "It was my fault. It was my idea—"

"Never mind. We'll discuss it later. It's time to go home. Thank you, Mr. McPherson." Mama shakes his hand and then she shakes Billy O'Connor's hand. "Thank you both for watching out for my family."

As we get into the car without a word, Daddy asks, "Where's Emmett?"

Mama kisses Daddy on the cheek. "He'll be home for Thanksgiving, Tom." She turns to look at us and says, "I'll deal with you two at home."

I climb into the backseat with Louise, wondering, did I dream this day? Is President Kennedy really gone? Will we start at some new school in Enka come January? How will Mama punish us? The air of the November night smells brisk and cold, and the sky is an inky black with a quilt of shining stars. Patsy Cline sings "Walking After Midnight" low on the radio. I love my Maggie Valley mountain home, and I want to keep it more than anything in the world, so on the quiet ride home, I think of the next letter that I will write to Mr. Flowers in December. It has to have Christmas spirit and not show any hint of desperation. I will write:

Dear Mr. George Flowers,

Merry Christmas. And Happy New Year. Thanks again for your nice words on my tune called "Louisiana's Song." I have oodles more songs to write for you. And you'll be happy to know that Daddy is playing the banjo again. I'm saving my money for a Trailways bus ticket to Nashville, Tennessee. The round-trip ticket costs $28.50, and I've almost got all the money saved up. I'm not sure of my exact travel dates, but I look forward to making your acquaintance and laying eyes on Music City USA in 1964. Have a very Merry Christmas, Mr. Flowers. Bye for now.

Sincerely, Olivia Hyatt Weems

Acknowledgments

"Your family in California is going to have to learn to spare you, so you can come soak up more stories of our mountains," Ernestine Upchurch told me on our way to the National Storytelling Festival in Jonesborough, Tennessee. And so since the publication of *Gentle's Holler*, I have found every opportunity to return to the Smoky Mountains to work on more stories of the Weems family.

I would like to thank Ernestine Upchurch and Popcorn Sutton for their generosity in providing a cabin for me to work on my Maggie Valley novels. I would also like to thank Valerie Privett, who offered her cabin in Townsend, Tennessee, where I found scratchy mountain music tapes that took me to another time and place when I wrote what would become *Louisiana's Song*.

I am very grateful to my editor, Catherine Frank, who saw more stories in Livy Two Weems and made me go deeper into the narrative of this mountain family to get to the heart and soul of *Louisiana's Song*. I would also like to thank Regina Hayes for giving my Maggie Valley novels a home with Viking Children's Books. And a very heartfelt thanks to my agent, Marianne Merola, at Brandt & Hochman, who patiently listened to titles, plots, and helped me see the bigger picture.

I would like to thank Dot Connor, who introduced me to her ninety-two-year mother, Mary Jane Queen of Jackson County, where I was able to visit a cabin over a hundred years old with a woodstove and water running right into the sink from the spring and listen to Mary Jane sing the old mountain ballads on her back porch and laugh her rich and beautiful laugh.

I am also grateful for the haunting voice of Sheila Kay Adams and the films of Neil Hutcheson that capture the stories of "Mountain Talk," and to Catherine Landis for her friendship and for telling me which Appalachian writers are the "real deal."

Without the help of my publicity angel, Rahni Sadler, I am quite certain far fewer kids would have found *Gentle's Holler*. And a huge thanks to Lori Special, children's librarian extraordinaire, who set up a week of writing workshops in Haywood County.

I would also like to express my deep thanks to Nashville singer and songwriter Tomi Lunsford, my sister-in-law, who took my lyrics and made them into the most beautiful mountain melodies. I would like to thank the three beautiful Lunsford sisters—Brenda Lilly Lunsford, Gail Lunsford, and Sandy Lunsford—for their generosity, laughter, and stories. I would also like to thank Logan Lark, who painted beautiful portraits of Uncle Hazard and the Weems kids, and said, "Tell the kids Louise did it!"

My brilliant Web site designer and brother-in-law, Ian Kovalik, has created a place of beauty for kids to explore. I also would to thank my mother and father, who gave me a childhood of moving around to football towns, which launched me into a life of "soaking up stories."

I am immensely grateful to my writers' group for the loving friendship, support, and encouragement along the way: Donna Rifkind, Diana Wagman, Heather Dundas, Diane Arieff, Denise Hamilton, and Lienna Silver. I would also especially like to thank Ellen Slezak for her generosity in both early and late manuscript stages.

I am grateful to Becky Fein's insight and honesty in helping me learn more about brain injuries and her amazing book recommendations: *Over My Head* by Claudia L. Osborn and *I'll Carry the Fork* by Kara L. Swanson.

I am sincerely grateful to Diana Budd and the students and faculty at the Frances Blend School for the Visually Impaired. I would also like to extend my deepest appreciation to Mr. Chris Persel, Director of Rehabilitation, and Dr. Mark Ashley, who allowed me to visit the Centre for Neuro Skills in Bakersfield, California, in the spring of 2006. I am very grateful to Sammi Flax, who suggested that Emmett whittle a cane for Gentle.

I would like to thank the people of Maggie Valley, especially Brenda O'Keefe at Joey's Pancake House, Evelyn White for all her stories about Ghost Town in the Sky, and Shirley Pinto for her Maggie Valley history. I am very grateful to Shirley Fairchild of the Opry House and her husband, Raymond Fairchild. I would also like to thank Louise Nelson, whose book, *Historic Waynesville*, was a great help.

I would like to thank Tina Hanlon of Ferrum College and her wonderful AppLit Web site; Poet Laureate Kathryn Stripling Byer, for her support of writers in North Carolina; David Cecelski for his article, "Book Dreams," on bookmobile driver Myrtle Peele; Karen Kreitzburg of Waynesville Middle School for sharing her stories of growing up in Crabtree; Meredith Tucker for sharing her Ghost Town in the Sky pictures and stories of Tennessee cousins growing up on the farm; and Nicki Nye and Debbie Jones for their book tour hospitality.

I will close expressing deep gratitude to my daughter Lucy, who was the voice of reason and got out the whiteboard and said, "Tell me the story. Start with chapter one." I would like to thank my son, Flannery, whose notes as an editor always pack a powerful punch to make the story stronger. And I would like to thank my youngest daughter, Norah, who loves fairies, butterflies, lightning bugs, and more stories—always more stories.

Finally, I thank my husband, Kiffen Madden-Lunsford, who is my heart and joy. I am so grateful to my mother-in-law, Frances Lunsford, who is pure courage and strength, and I will forever marvel at her raising thirteen children with her husband, Jim, a man I never met but feel like I know a little bit.

Property of:

Redwood Middle School Library

200 Doherty Drive

Larkspur, CA 94939